START

MW00958133

Austin Bates
© 2018
Disclaimer

This book contains sexually explicit content that is intended for ADULTS ONLY (+18).

Chapter 1 - Martin

A Chihuahua defeated me today. I tried my best, but I still wasn't able to overcome my fear.

The dog stared me down from across the aisle. I knew it couldn't hurt me. Damn little thing probably weighed less than 5 pounds. It had bugged-out eyes, and curly fur coming out of its ears, and its tail curled like a pig's. I should have had no problem petting it, or even approaching it enough for it to sniff me.

Instead, I stood there in one spot and stared at it until the owner noticed me. I immediately stammered out a question, one of those standard can-I-help-you questions everyone knows.

I think I gave her a weird vibe, because she only looked at me and then scooped up her dog and hurried off. And when that Chihuahua peered over her shoulder at me, I looked away and went back to stocking dog toys, like I'd been doing in the first place before I sensed an actual dog was nearby.

Now, thinking back on it, frustration rose up inside me and I slapped my hand against the steering wheel. The wheel hadn't cooled off yet from sitting out in the sun in the parking lot all day, so all I did was succeed in burning myself.

Hissing, I put the injured part of my palm in my mouth and sucked to try and ease the pain. My heart was heavy enough already, and this minor wound was just adding insult to injury.

A person working at a pet store shouldn't be afraid of dogs. It would have been okay if I was scared of the snakes or tarantulas; those weren't common pets. I didn't have to deal with them, if I could get someone else to do it.

Except I was a backwards idiot who had no problem dealing with creepy crawlies. It was the fluffy, barking variety of pet I couldn't handle.

I was afraid of dogs. For an understandable reason, maybe, but it was putting a dent in my lifestyle, and I needed to get over it soon, or else I was risking the career I wanted.

I *wanted* to overcome it. I really, really did. So I tried with every dog I saw.

Usually, the outcome was the same as today's. If the dog stared, waiting, I felt creeping unease gnawing its way up my spine, and I backed down.

If the dog charged for me, like so many excitable pets do, I didn't even really have a chance to feel that unease before I fled. My body reacted before my thoughts could catch up, not that my brain was much use in these kinds of situations.

Another day, another failure. How much longer can I keep kidding myself?

I put my hand back down on the steering wheel, which had cooled off enough by now to be bearable. I drove through Red Bluff, heading home after my long, miserable, unsuccessful day, and tried to think of other things besides my failures — and what my parents would think of me.

Maybe I should relax. Go for a drive, get a drink. Meet a man and take him home.

Someone nice and proper, of course. I'd read enough horror stories on Reddit to be wary of burly alpha males.

As I kept driving, the idea started to solidify in my mind. It wasn't half-bad, really. I'd have some fun, some sex, and I wouldn't be thinking at all about my stupid job, or my stupid fears, or my stupid…

A strange cloud in the sky caught my attention, putting a halt to my moody thoughts. I took my foot off the gas pedal and bent over a little to peer through the windshield, too fascinated to care about proper driving. The cloud was a vast, shifting gray mass of wisps and curls, dissipating and growing all at the same time. Its bulk trailed down, growing narrower as it went — the shape of a tornado.

I couldn't see where the source of the cloud was because of trees and houses in the distance.

The source…

Because it wasn't a cloud at all.

My fascination changed to horror as I realized I was looking at a plume of smoke, seeping across the sky like a stain. The pure blue of the early evening turned hazy and pallid while I watched.

Car horns started to beep and blast behind me. I didn't look at them, couldn't care less about the traffic I was creating.

There was a fire. Here. In Red Bluff.

California might be infamous for its apocalyptic blazes, but there had never been a big fire here in the past. Plus, the Sacramento River was nearby. It seemed wrong for a fire of this apparent size to exist so near a source of water.

All the same, there it was.

That's in the direction of my neighborhood.

Everything seemed suddenly much more real. I stomped on the gas again and felt my car give a few jittery lurches before catching itself and finally speeding up. The cars behind me, which had been looming so large in my rearview mirror, now fell away as I put distance between us.

Far off, beneath the blasting roar of the air-conditioning, I heard the distinctive *honk* of a fire engine. The sound was like a first domino, setting off a long string of warnings and alarms in my brain.

I turned off the main road without using my signal and drove way too fast down the street, ignoring several stop signs. I turned left and then right another few streets down, still without using my signal.

My neighborhood was right in front of me now, rows of houses. Mine was over in the back of the area, near a disused railroad track surrounded by scrubby trees and bushes.

The poisonous cloud of black smoke was almost right overhead. Many of my neighbors were outside, standing in their yards, or walking along the sidewalk to try and see what was going on. The blaring of sirens and fire engine *honks* were much louder, and I thought I could also hear shouting.

I drove as fast as I could through the chaos, prepared to go all the way down to my home, when red-and-blue lights flashed behind me.

Chapter 2 - Lance

I knew we were going to get a call for a fire before it even happened. I'd known for hours, and it wasn't just because this was the hottest day of the year so far. Today had been set in motion a long time ago, and this was just a consequence of that.

Anticipation made me tense. Even though I wasn't assigned to any chores, I had picked up a broom about an hour ago and I had been sweeping ever since. Room after room, passing the rough bristles over the floor in a steady rhythm.

My hands felt sore, like I might be getting a blister from clutching the handle so tight. Fuck it. Blisters were nothing when compared with the beast of burden on my back, this knowledge of what was going to happen. If anything, the pain helped distract me.

The dinner bell rang, chiming throughout the fire station. I kept my head down, kept sweeping while the others left their work and headed to the kitchen to see what was waiting for them. I knew about that, too.

I'd helped chop carrots and celery and chicken for the stew earlier in the day, which had been simmering in a pot on the stove since then. The sweet, yeasty scent of bread that drifted through the air told me someone had been doing some baking. Rolls or biscuits with our stew.

Good, hearty food for hungry men.

My stomach turned at the thought of eating. I'd looked forward to it earlier, but things had changed since then. A fire was brewing, building, gathering strength while everyone else went about their business with no clue.

"Hey, Lance."

I looked up at the familiar voice and grunted at the man approaching me. "Shep."

Shepherd was just about my best friend here at the station, though that wasn't saying much. It wasn't something I'd volunteered for, either. He'd attached himself to me, and that was that. Nothing much else to it, really.

Shep nodded at the broom. "You coming to dinner? I hear you had a hand in it, yeah?"

I grunted again and went back to sweeping. Get a bunch of men tromping around in big boots and soon enough, you'd have a lot of mess to clean up. The pile of dirt I was gathering was more of a mountain, studded with twigs and leaves and a few smashed clumps of what might have been dried rabbit shit.

No mistaking rabbit shit, not for a country boy. Looks like Cocoa Puffs.

Shep didn't move away, which was pretty much in line with his character. The guy didn't know when to leave well enough alone.

"Yeah," I finally said. "Yeah, I helped. Just cut vegetables up, though."

"Even that makes it taste better. You should be our cook all the time."

"Thanks. Grew up on a farm. You can't be a farm boy without learning how to cook what comes from the ground."

"You just proved my point. So, you coming?"

"No."

Shep frowned a little. "Do you feel okay? You've been acting weird for the past couple of months."

I lifted my head again and stared right at him. He looked back at me with his big ol' blue eyes, which were innocent and bright.

Shep was the only person in the entire fire department who could look me right in the eye when I glared at him. It wasn't because he was braver than anyone else, no. He was just too nice to realize when someone was trying to intimidate him.

"I just have off days, like everyone else. That okay with you?"

"Maybe if you'd relax a little and come sit down with everyone else, you'd feel better."

My shoulders slumped. "Thanks, but no. You go on, Shep. Maybe I'll join everyone tomorrow. For now, I got some thinking to do, and I do that best while I'm moving."

Shep shrugged. It was different when he shrugged than when anyone else did. Instead of pushing something aside, his shrug seemed to be more of an acceptance. Like, he couldn't do something about this, so, okay, he'd let it go for now. "Maybe you'll play cards later tonight, then."

"Yeah. Maybe later tonight," I echoed.

Later tonight, the fire would be out, and I could relax. I'd need to relax, to get rid of the guilt.

Right now, I had to work and wait for the reveal.

Barely two minutes passed after Shepherd left before the alarm went off. This bell was sharper, higher-pitched, an echoing clang that could be heard in every room of the station.

It's early, I thought. That didn't mean much. Someone could have stumbled across the fire before they were meant to. I was glad for that, some of the tension inside me easing. It'd be easier to take care of, this way.

When the alarm ended, a voice came over the speaker system. A computerized voice, like Siri. "Fire spotted near Tehama County Fairgrounds. Available units, report to scene."

But that wasn't right. The fire shouldn't have been near there. It should have been to the north, near Paynes Creek

Road. Where it was now was too close to people, to houses. Lives were at risk, if that was true.

Maybe the person who called the fire in had gotten the location wrong. I hoped for that, but I knew deep in my heart the solution couldn't be so easy.

Dropping the broom, I ran down the hall and took a few turns until I reached the map room, where everyone else had already gathered. Shep was there, and Bailey and Chris, and at least a dozen others.

Plus the chief, standing at the head of the room.

Chief Patrick acted like he hadn't noticed me. He held a pointing stick in his hand, like the kind professors use in college lectures. He tapped the point of his stick near the fairgrounds. "The fire has been spotted here." If anyone noticed the slight tension at the corner of his mouth, or the way his eyes flickered, they didn't comment on it.

Me, I noticed. And I knew there was going to be hell to pay when this was done with.

"No reports on the size of it," Chief Patrick said. "But the way it's so near a lot of communities, we can't take a chance. Two teams, two engines." He gestured with his stick to half of us. "Take number one. The rest of you, take four. This will be our route. Optimal positioning near hydrants in the area are here, here, and here."

It was all so normal, as normal as any other call. The chief was in control, and everyone else hung on his every word, noting what he said, the route he outlined, the places he pointed out for us. There was nothing to show that things were different, since only he and I would know anything about that.

"Everyone got that? Good. Get into your gear and head out. I'll get some of the part-timers to come in and cover the place while you're out."

That was standard. If we were out on an important call, someone had to be around to handle anything else that came in, even if it was as minor as getting a cat out of a tree.

Along with everyone else, I headed into the gear room and pulled on my suit, zipping zippers and pulling straps tight until it felt like I was wearing a heavy second skin instead of clothing. The extra weight helped to ground me some, calmed my breathing.

No matter the circumstances, this was routine. This was normal. We'd get this shit licked and be back home in time for dessert and a few hands of poker.

I stayed back in the gear room, helping my brothers and sisters with a tricky strap here and there where they couldn't reach. Once all of us were ready, with only a few minutes having passed, we split up into our two teams and headed for our respective engines.

I was on four. Shep, thankfully, wound up on engine one. Two and three were out of rotation for maintenance work. They *could* be used, but the rotation helped us better keep up with wear and tear.

My team piled onto the fire engine. Our driver pulled out of the garage, flipped on the bright red flashing lights that would alert traffic to our presence, and honked the horn. Then we were on our way.

Being in the back of a fire engine felt a bit like riding in the back of an ambulance. All of us were bounced around and jostled like rocks in a tumbler. The wheels of the engine hardly ever seemed to touch the ground, like we were skipping on the surface of a lake instead of driving on hard concrete.

Everyone else clung to handholds, gripped the walls, talking in soft, hushed voices. The usual chatter. The newer firefighters repeated information to themselves, trying to remember all of it so they wouldn't look stupid. The veterans amongst us gave advice and talked strategy.

All the other veterans did, anyway. Not me. I just held onto my handle, kept my feet on the ground, and tried not to look as confused as I felt. If someone looked at me and thought too hard about my odd behavior, I was as good as done for.

All of this could still be a fluke, a mistake, but I stopped trying to believe in that right around the time I got my first whiff of smoke. There was a woodsy smell to it, like a campfire. Trees were burning.

There weren't supposed to be any trees involved.

There was no way of knowing what was going on in the outside world, aside from what we could feel and hear. Our driver honked several times, probably trying to clear out a path ahead of us. We made several wide turns at fast speeds, and then we started to slow. Getting closer to our destination.

A speaker came on, our driver using his microphone. "Get ready," he said. "Helmets on. It looks like a bad one."

My heart sank. I did as I was told, then helped the others with theirs.

The engine came to a stop, a full stop, and in the quiet that followed, I was able to hear a distinctive, familiar, terrifying sound. It was low, nearly inaudible. A muted roaring, like the sound of waves beating on the ocean shore.

It was the sound of an uncontrolled blaze.

"Dammit," I whispered. My voice was muffled by the helmet, and no one heard me. We all headed for the door and pulled it open, then hopped out.

Going from the dim interior of an enclosed vehicle to the brightness of outside made me squint. I waited for my eyes to adjust.

Someone whistled, the sound long and low and appreciative. "Hot damn. Would you look at that?"

I stood in the middle of the street, surrounded by park-type scenery. Grass sliced through with walking paths, threaded with trees. Through the trees, I could see houses and apartment buildings in the distance. Everything looked pretty normal, like a regular evening just before dusk made itself known.

The heat at my back told me things were *not* normal.

Slowly, with a sense of impending doom, I turned around.

It was like Hell had burst up out of the ground and was on the verge of reclaiming the living world. Bright orange-yellow flames crawled all over the fields near the fairgrounds. Grass turned black in massive, spreading patches. Tongues of fire licked their way from the top of one tree to the next, spreading rapidly. Smoke turned the sky black, casting a massive shadow on the ground. Ash and soot swirled through the air like dirty snow, blown on drafts of scorching heat.

What had I done?

How the hell had things advanced to this stage? This wasn't...

No time to think about that. Act, not react.

I turned back to the fire engine and joined everyone else in the quick prep to get this handled. Together, we unwound the hose and worked out the trajectory, the best place to blast. Marked the position of the fire hydrant, just in case we needed more than what we were carrying.

All fires worked in a similar manner. They wanted to burn, and they couldn't do that when they were doused with water. Drench the flames, drench the surrounding area, and that would be the end of the terrifying display.

Yeah, it wasn't going to be that easy.

Chapter 3 - Lance

It took several of us to hold the hose in position as thousands of gallons of water came bursting out the nozzle, spraying through the air with incredible power. The roar of the water momentarily drowned out the snarling of the fire, and some of the flames fizzled and died where moisture touched them.

Relief formed in my chest. My arms ached from holding the hose, my hands burning. It was difficult to see, with flying droplets of water mingling with soot to form a muddy, greasy coating on the glass surface of my face mask.

We moved the hose, aiming to hit the base of the fire to really do some damage. The second we did, the flames jumped right back into the space where they had just been extinguished.

A rapid hissing noise joined the roars, and the snarling, crackling sounds, and it sent a chill down my spine, despite the oven-like nature of the air. That was the sound of evaporation. All the water we had just poured onto this fire was being gasified by the extreme heat, rendering it useless.

"Hit the base!"

The other team, from engine one, finally got their hose prepped. A second stream of gushing water joined the first, deafening, painful to hear. The battle raged, two primeval forces contending for dominance.

After a short time, it came clear that one of these forces was much stronger than the other.

I turned my head and shouted, "Bailey!"

Nothing.

I couldn't get to my walkie, not with both hands clamped on the hose.

"Bailey!" I roared, putting everything I had into it. The shout formed deep in my chest, bursting out of me. I sounded like a furious bear. Someone on the line behind me flinched. The tiny movement caused a butterfly effect, jerking the hose, jerking me, causing the nozzle to shift. A centimeter turned into several feet of difference in the direction of the water shooting through the air, and flames lunged up to fill the space which had just been left unoccupied.

Miraculously, Bailey appeared at my side. He wasn't exactly a veteran, but neither was he a new guy. He knew enough to keep his shit together, basically.

"Yeah, Lance?" He had to yell to be heard, even standing a foot away from me.

"We need the other engines. Get the chief on the radio. Get number three, if that's all we can get. Get in touch with the cops. Get these roads blocked off."

Bailey disappeared again and I couldn't track where he went, focused as I was on the job at hand.

By the time the third engine arrived, both of our teams had switched to using the hydrants. The police showed up and began redirecting traffic, blocking off access to the nearby neighborhoods. I hoped and hoped that we wouldn't have to resort to an evacuation.

Hope was a desperate thing. Smoke completely filled the sky overhead, making it seem like it was already nighttime. The rotating and flashing lights of the fire engines and the police cars played across the plumes of smoke; the shapes of the flames made it seem as though Hell was throwing a rave.

Try as we might to diminish the fire or stop its spreading, we couldn't. Every inch of progress we won was eaten by a foot of flame. Water alone was not going to be enough.

We needed some heavy-duty extinguishers and some blockades. We needed more than this.

All of this was all my fault.

As the minutes dragged on and the situation grew worse, I had to admit to myself that someone needed to make the call. That someone had to be me.

I was replaced on the hose, letting someone fresher hold my position. Gritting my teeth, I went up to the front of engine four and reached for the radio. The chief picked up as soon as I was able to put in the call to him, like he'd been sitting there waiting for this.

"Chief," I said. "We need to evacuate."

"Why?"

Frustration and fear formed a hard knot in my throat. I choked around it, sputtered, managed to find my voice. "I don't know *why*. I don't know what went wrong here. I do know there are dozens of homes around, and they are all way too damn close. This smoke is..."

"I'll take your word for it," Chief Patrick said, cutting me off. "I trust your judgment. Evacuate the two nearest neighborhoods, put out an alert for the others. Then put the damn fire out. Don't you dare disappoint me, Lance."

He ended the transmission, his last few words disappearing into a burst of static. I stared at the radio, growled, then threw the mouthpiece against the dashboard and hopped out of the engine. The chief's words were like poison in my ears, weakening me, making me want to give in.

I couldn't.

After giving word to some of my brothers, along with instructions to pass the news around, I headed over to the nearest police officer, who sat in his cruiser with a look of pants-pissed terror on his face. Seemed kind of strange to me how a man could face abuse and cruelty, get shot at, stabbed at, punched, could have all these awful things happen to him, and still be so afraid of a fire.

Fire could be understood. People, not so much.

The officer climbed out of his cruiser and faced me, clearly trying to stand tall and look as impressive as his uniform and badge demanded. His badge said his name was Perkins.

"How is everything, sir?" he asked.

I guessed that was a fair question to ask. Covered every topic, and I could answer it however I liked. I cut to the chase, since I couldn't much tolerate beating around the bush.

"There needs to be an evacuation. This entire area is at risk. The two nearest neighborhoods have got to be cleared out, right here, right now."

In the grand scheme of things, cops outrank firefighters. However, in terms of experience and dominance, I outranked this fresh-faced officer. His hands trembled and his chin shook before he got himself under control and nodded. "I'll put the request through."

"No." I stared Perkins down, glaring into his eyes and piercing him straight through. He shrank back, his eyes going wide and white-rimmed, like a terrified horse. He wasn't immune to me like Shep was. "This is not a request. This is an order. There are lives at stake here."

"I'll put the order through," Perkins whispered.

I didn't stick around to say anything else. I got back to work.

I kept an eye and an ear on the evacuation process. Perkins apparently got the approval for it, and more police cars started to arrive, a few of which were from different counties. Officers swarmed around like crazed ants, making announcements using their speakers, knocking on individual doors. People burst out of their houses, throwing armfuls of random supplies into their vehicles before driving away as fast as they could.

At some point, I found myself on evacuation duty, assisting with the process. I helped guide older folks, carried heavy items, watched kids, and held leashed dogs. Anything that needed doing, it became my job to do.

It was while I was holding a dog leash and a covered bird cage that I saw something in the corner of my vision that demanded my attention. A white car, turned beige with a layer of dust and dirt, drove up and then pulled over to the curb with a police car right up on his back bumper. Rather than wait for the officer in the cruiser to come to him, the driver of the car pushed his door open and stepped out.

Even from a block away, it was obvious that the driver of the car was a cute guy. Tousled golden hair, slim figure. He gestured around with his hands while speaking, paused for a moment to listen to what the cop had to say, and then resumed gesturing around. His face showed extreme distress, not that I could blame him. It had to suck to come home only to be turned away.

The family who owned the animals I was holding onto came over and took them from me.

"Need anything else?" I asked, turning my attention back to them.

When the answer was no, I made sure they got out of their driveway safely and was about to go over to help the family at the next house when I heard a despairing shout. "But I don't have anywhere else to go!"

I turned and saw the cute guy with his arms spread out wide. I couldn't see much of his expression from so far away, but his posture was that of a man begging. The cop looked torn between exasperation, pity, and anger.

He understood the situation, felt for the little guy, but he also probably wasn't used to being disobeyed, and that, combined with the situation, had him on edge. His hackles were up, his back straight, shoulders squared.

Before I knew it, something had me crossing the street, heading in the direction of that dirty car and the cute guy leaning up against it as if his legs had given out. Maybe it was because I knew I could intimidate an omega, and many alphas, into doing what they were supposed to. Or I felt guilty, and wanted to be there for the confrontation.

Or maybe it was because I'd always had a thing for omegas with blond hair.

As I came up on them, the omega lifted his head from his hands and looked at me. His eyes were dark brown, startlingly deep, and shiny as ink. He was even cuter close up, with a button nose, rounded face, and pink, pouty lips that looked as if they were just begging to be kissed. One ear was pierced with a diamond stud, which caught and reflected the dancing light of the distant flames.

"Are you a firefighter?" he asked. His voice was rough. Either he'd strained it shouting, he smoked, or he was holding back a lot of emotions. Judging from the liquid brightness of his eyes, it was probably that last one.

Looking at him, I felt my awareness of the nearby police officer fade away. I knew he was standing there, watching, but he didn't matter compared to this slender cutie.

"Yeah, I am," I said, surprising myself by not being sarcastic. "You okay? Something going on?"

"Can't you tell me what's going on?" he asked, his voice pleading. "Where did this come from? Why can't I go home?"

I decided to skip the middle question, since even I didn't really know the answer to that at the moment. "Yeah, I can tell you what's going on. These two areas are being evacuated.

"It's too dangerous to be this close to the fire. Smoke could get you, if nothing else. You can't go home. The only reason you got this close is because the barricades aren't all in place yet."

"But you guys are here. You're putting the fire out. It should be safe, shouldn't it?"

I bit my tongue to keep from grimacing. "We're doing the best we can to restore order. You don't have anything to worry about, so you can just leave this to us."

Soothing words did nothing for the guy. He shook his head, his hands twisting over each other in a wringing motion. "I was trying to tell this officer here that I can't. I can't leave. I don't have anywhere else to go."

That was what I'd heard him shout. The repetition of it now, combined with the look on his face, told me that he wasn't just being dramatic. My stomach twisted with sympathy and I found myself moving closer to him, until I felt the warmth of his body through my suit even more clearly than I had felt the heat of the fire.

Though the choking smell of wood smoke stained every breath, I could smell him. Faint cologne, like it had worn off throughout the day, leaving a lingering sweetness. Something else I couldn't identify, an animal sort of scent.

I wanted to touch him, to put my hand on his knee. I held back, knowing that I looked even more intimidating than usual when I was in my suit. He was scared enough already. "What's your name, buddy?"

"Martin," he said.

"That's a good name. A strong name. Martin, I'm Lance."

A ghost of a smile briefly haunted his pouting lips. "Lance is an even stronger name."

"I guess it is," I said. "Martin, what do you mean when you say you have nowhere else to go?"

Martin pointed. I turned and looked in that direction, didn't see anything except one of the neighborhoods currently being evacuated. "I live over there. It's just me. I don't have any relatives nearby, or a boyfriend I can stay with, or anything."

He said boyfriend.

Making note of that, though I wasn't sure why, I asked, "Got any friends you can stay with?"

He shrugged. "Not really. I've got friends, but no one I'd ask to live with."

"You're going to have to," the police officer interjected, reminding me he was still there. I stared at him, silencing him, and turned back to Martin.

"What about a hotel?"

Martin lifted one shoulder in a hopeless shrug. "I could afford it for a few nights, but I really couldn't, you know? Do you think this is going to last longer than a few days?"

He looked at me as if I had all the answers. I pulled in a short, sharp breath, held it, and then let it out shakily. "We'll do the best we can to put the fire out as soon as possible."

It wasn't a real answer, and he knew it. His expression darkened and he stared down at his hands, defeated.

By this point, I was very aware of how much time was passing while I had this conversation. There were many others still who could use my help, and soon I would have to go back to relieve someone on the hoses.

Seconds ticked by, my heart keeping up with a double rhythm. This problem *needed* to be solved.

There was really only one solution. This fire was my fault. This mistake was also somehow my fault.

Therefore, everything else was on my shoulders. The evacuation, Martin's lack of a place to stay. If I wanted to fix this, I had to atone for my mistake.

Basically, I was giving in to the guilt, like I always gave up so easily in the face of blackmail.

"You can stay at my place," I said.

Martin stared at me, his mouth opening slightly. He shook his head, tried to say something, and ended up gawking again.

"If you've got nowhere to go and you can't afford a hotel, I can let you stay in my house until the fire's out. It isn't much to look at, but it's better than being homeless." I tried to smile, to let him know I was teasing him.

If he noticed, he didn't care. He pushed up off the hood of his car, his jaw still slack. "Are you serious?"

"I am," I said, and at that point I couldn't go back even if I'd wanted to. I'd committed myself to this. "Decide fast. I gotta get back to working as soon as I can."

"I couldn't…"

I interrupted. "You could, and you will. Look, I'd feel like I failed my job if I let you go off without knowing you were safe. This way, we both get what we need. Yeah?"

I watched indecision and doubt play across his face. His shoulders slumped and he pushed his hand through his hair, silky curls wrapping around his fingers and tumbling down over his forehead. "Okay. Thank you. Thank you so much, Firefighter Lance."

"Just call me Lance," I said.

The cop who'd been watching us up until now cleared his throat and stepped back. "Guess you got this figured out. I'll get back to my own work, then."

He headed back to his cruiser, and I was pretty sure I detected relief in the way he was walking. One problem down, fifty thousand more to go.

Looking back at Martin, I held out my hand. "We got us a deal?"

Martin grabbed at my gloved hand with both of his and squeezed tightly. "Thank you. Thank you so, so much."

Something happened to me as he held my hand like that, even though I couldn't feel his skin. I could still feel the pressure of his fingers, the strength of the gesture. My stomach fluttered with a sudden weightlessness, like vertigo.

I don't understand how he's single. He should have a husband and five kids.

Pulling my hand away, I grunted, "Let me tell the others where I'm going, then we'll stop by your place *very quickly.* Throw some clothes together, whatever you need.

"Then I'll take you to my house. Gonna need to take your car with me when I leave, though, so I can get back here. I'll park it somewhere safe. Got it?"

Martin nodded. He rubbed his hands together, like they were cold. His cheeks were flushed from the hot, oppressive air. "Got it."

"Stay here."

I headed back over to the fire engines, searching for someone I could pull aside and deliver the news to. With each step I took away from Martin, concern replaced my convictions.

Inviting this guy into my home put him that much closer to me and the secrets I kept. I would have to be very careful with him. I couldn't let him draw me in any further, not out of my own guilt, and not out of sympathy, and especially not because his big brown eyes beseeched me to do so.

Spying Shep, I changed course and went to him to tell him my plan.

Some people might have said what I was doing went above and beyond the call of duty. For other firefighters, yeah, maybe so. We usually didn't leave the scene of an emergency for anything.

For me, this wasn't just anything. I couldn't do enough to help these people I'd wronged. I would do everything I could, one person at a time.

Chapter 4 - Martin

As if today couldn't get any worse, now I was blocked from going home to relax and unwind. I guess I shouldn't have been surprised. The scene in front of me was literally chaos, even worse than what I'd seen on my way here.

The smoke was as thick as thunderheads, the flickers of fire like flashes of lightning. Sirens blipped and emergency lights spun and pulsed from the roofs of police cars, fire trucks, and ambulances. Emergency workers in various uniforms, ranging from white to blue, milled around, directing traffic, guiding people, and blocking entrances and exits.

The combined force of all the different voices made it sound as if I was standing in the middle of a stadium, instead of a suburban street.

If it wasn't for Firefighter Lance, I didn't know what I would have done. Everything I'd told him was true. I had no boyfriend, no real, true friends I felt comfortable calling up. My parents were several states away, and no way in hell was I going to rely on them at a time like this. That would only reinforce their low opinion of me.

Lance was saving my life. He'd come out of the smoke like some burly avenging angel, moving in his bulky suit as if it were made of paper. I hadn't been able to see much of his body except to notice how broad he was, easily as wide as two of me. He was also tall, towering over me like a statue.

He had a rugged face, made up of wide curves and sharp lines, like a movie star. I hadn't been able to see what color his eyes were, or his hair, because of his helmet.

I really wanted to know.

When I'd grabbed his hand, I had been able to feel how big it was. The bulk of the glove was hiding a broad palm and thick fingers. He could probably wrap his one hand all the way around my neck.

Damn, that had kick-started something inside me. It was an awful time to get aroused, or to even *think* about being turned on, but it had happened anyway, and I blushed. Luckily, he didn't seem to have noticed.

Lance came back now, after talking to another firefighter. He flipped up the front part of his mask, which I guessed was mostly there to help him see better. It probably sucked to try and fight a fire when there was so much soot and ash in your face that you couldn't see.

"We're good to go," Lance growled. "Let's get this show on the road, okay? Drive fast. No one's going to care about speeding right now."

The sound of his voice made me shiver. I nodded and grabbed my car keys from my pocket. "I'm ready."

Lance opened the passenger side door of my car, and I got in behind the wheel. My hand shook while I tried to get the key into the ignition, metal clicking against metal.

Lance made a sound under his breath. It might have been impatience, or maybe it was just a sound. Either way, it gave me the kick in the ass I needed to find the hole and jab the key in.

My car stuttered to life, shaking and bouncing briefly before settling down. My heart pounding in my ears, I put both hands on the steering wheel and gripped tightly. I pulled away from the chaotic scene, heading for the deeper areas of the neighborhood.

The first thing I noticed was the fire. I was driving parallel to it now, its full scale revealed to me. Everything was covered in orange and red and yellow flame, which swooped across the ground, raced up trees, leapt from branch to branch with unnerving speed. The fire seemed distinctly alive, like an apex hunter gone crazy.

A warm touch on my hand made me turn my head. Lance pulled my hand on the steering wheel. "Stay in your lane," he chided.

I blushed, feeling like a high schooler out on their first drive. I focused back on the road again, trying to ignore the flames covering the entire left side of my field of vision.

Lance sighed. "It's something else, isn't it?"

"It's terrifying," I whispered.

I saw Lance nod in my peripheral vision. "Yeah. It is that. That's why you have to get away from here."

I hadn't really understood until now how bad things were. I hadn't known fire could move so fast. I hadn't seen how close the nearest house was to all this.

I drove a little faster, urgency rising inside me like the tide.

We reached my house in record time. I lived in a little place not much bigger than a trailer, though it was an actual house. The siding was painted blue, and the roofing was gray.

I'd done my best with the gardening. Even if the lawn wasn't mowed in the straightest manner, at least I had some pretty flowers on the porch. It wasn't the best place to live, but I could afford to live there, and it was mine. That was all that mattered to me.

Now my little house was shadowed by smoke, the walls already going gray with soot carried over on the wind.

"Go in, grab a bag. When you come out, I'll take you to my place." Lance repeated the plan, as if I needed reminding.

I guess I did need reminding, because I hadn't moved an inch since coming to a stop in front of my driveway. Regret and trepidation weighed heavy on my shoulders, threatening to crush me. Trying to shake all that away, I got out of the car and ran inside.

Did Lance watch me run the whole way there, or was I only imagining the feel of his eyes burning into me?

I grabbed the doorknob and threw the door open, then headed back to my bedroom and grabbed a backpack I kept in the closet. One of the straps was so worn that it looked as if it would snap if I tugged on it the right way. Or the wrong way.

Whatever. It would do.

I grabbed some clothes, my toothbrush and hairbrush and a few other toiletries, some books, a couple movies, my 3DS. When I still had room left over, I added more clothes on top. Then I stood there, thinking, debating.

Could I survive on this for days? Weeks? If my house burned down, would this be enough to keep me going until I found a new place to live?

I thought of everything I stood to lose. My decorations, my photographs. All the food in my fridge and pantries, bought and paid for. My appliances, my furniture. Mementos and games and knickknacks, some of which I'd kept around since I was a kid.

No amount of backpacks would ever be enough.

A car honked outside. I knew that sound well enough; Lance was summoning me.

Like a captive genie, doomed to do as he said, I slung my backpack over my shoulder and left the house. Lance was in the driver's seat now, gesturing for me to hurry up. I ran the last few paces and then threw myself inside, pulling my heavy backpack behind me.

Before I could close my door, Lance was already driving. I tugged the door shut and started to pull on my seatbelt.

"Looks like you got a good haul," Lance said.

I peeked over at him. The brim of his helmet still had his face hidden in shadows. The urge to know what he looked like without it was stronger than ever. I had to know the face of my hero. "I got the essentials."

"Yeah? You got soap in there?"

"No?" *Soap?*

"What about drinking water? Food? Matches? Toilet paper?"

"Do you live on a campground?" I asked, wondering if he was toying with me.

He grunted, which I thought might have been his way of laughing. "Yeah, a campground. That's funny.

"Just saying you aren't as prepared as you think you are. But it's fine. I'll let you use my toilet paper."

He really was teasing me. I could hardly believe it. At a time like this, a firefighter was teasing me.

Two could play at this game. "I'd like to use toilet paper you haven't used, please."

"Depends on how tough things get," he said. I laughed, and he let out another of those grunts.

Relaxing back in my seat while he drove, I let myself think that this might not be so bad after all. Lance might look like he was seven feet of alpha badass and aggression, but he clearly had a sense of humor. I could deal with this for a few days, though going home was still the better option, if I had to make a choice.

The drive to Lance's house took about 15 minutes, which were spent mostly in silence. He pulled up in front of a cookie-cutter house, which was a carbon copy of all the others around it. "This is it," he said.

"How can you tell?" I asked.

Lance chuckled. "You're cute. Come on, I'll let you in."

I'm cute?

Breathless, I followed him up to the front porch. He unlocked the door, then gestured me inside. "Can't really take the time to give you the grand tour. Look around. Help yourself to something in the fridge if you're hungry. I'll probably be back in the morning."

Lance turned away, reaching out to shut the door behind him. I grabbed his hand again, stopping him. My heart fluttered in my chest, beginning to rise into my throat with each beat. "Are you sure this is okay?" I asked. "For me to just … be here?"

Lance said nothing, and I thought he might be reconsidering his offer, about to tell me that no, it wasn't okay, go somewhere else, and good luck. Then he sighed and reached up to take off his helmet.

His eyes were turquoise, a perfect marriage of blue and green, framed by long, thick eyelashes. His hair was flattened and sweaty, either dark brown or black. I couldn't look away from him, couldn't move a muscle in my entire body as he leaned in until our noses were almost touching. I could taste his breath on my lips, which were tingling.

"It's fine. Just respect my boundaries, and we'll be good. Okay?"

"Okay," I whispered. My loins felt somehow tense and loose all at once.

Lance stayed near my face, and I thought he might kiss me. I wanted him to. I almost started leaning in.

He pulled away like he was forcing himself to do it and shut the door behind him. I listened to his receding steps as he headed back along the short walkway to the driveway. My car's engine purred clunkily, and I saw him back up and pull away.

Then I was all alone in this unfamiliar place. Things had gotten a lot more complicated, very quickly.

I pulled in a deep breath to try and steady myself, then let it out. Setting my backpack down by the front door, I went around Lance's house to give myself that tour.

First, there was the foyer. Nothing much to it, just an honest-to-god hat stand covered in hats, and a shoe rack covered in mainly boots. To the left, a staircase leading down to the basement. Judging from the musty smell coming from down there, it was an unfinished basement, most likely used for storage. Nothing of interest for me there.

In front of me was a living room, with a couch, an armchair, and a couple of side tables. An open, empty pizza box lay on the couch, and there were other dirty dishes and half-full cups lying around. Clutter, though not to the point of dirtiness.

That made me feel a little better. Lance was still an ordinary guy, one who didn't much like to clean up after himself.

Aside from the furniture, the living room had a flat-screen TV above a small entertainment system stocked with movies, all of which seemed to be classics or contemporary popular films. Maybe a busy firefighter didn't have the time or patience to comb through the world of indie movies and direct-to-DVD flops.

The living room led to a cluttered kitchen with dishes piled up in the sink. A laundry room and dining room were on either side.

Going back to the living room, I poked down the other direction and found a hallway with a single bedroom and a bathroom. The bathroom definitely looked like a guy used it. The tub needed scrubbing, there were signs of mold from too-humid showers on the ceiling, and the mirror above the sink was in need of a cleaning. The sink itself was sprinkled with a liberal dosage of hairs, short and curly.

I didn't look in the medicine cabinet, and I didn't even poke my head into the bedroom. What Lance had said about respecting his boundaries had really stuck with me. I was a guest in his home. I didn't need to go snooping around in places where I didn't belong, even though the sneak peeks into his life were fascinating.

Sighing, I went back to the living room and flopped on the couch. Nice, sturdy couch. The springs didn't so much as squeak beneath me. Laying my head back, I closed my eyes and tried to think about what my next step was going to be.

I could explore the fridge? Being around all that smoke and heat had made me pretty thirsty. Plus, it was past my regular dinnertime, and I was beginning to feel the dull, throbbing ache of hunger chewing at my stomach.

I should call the people I knew. My *acquaintances,* for lack of a better word, to see if they were aware of the fire and were safe. I could text my boss to alert him of my situation and ask if the animals at the shop were going to be okay.

Birds and rodents, especially, had fragile respiratory systems. If the smoke got bad enough, they could be in real danger.

Back up, I scolded myself. Anxiety was making me stupid. The pet shop wasn't anywhere near where I lived. The fire had seemed to be moving in the opposite direction, too. I shouldn't let myself jump to worst-case-scenario conclusions like that.

Naturally, my next thought was of the *worst* worst-case-scenario. Before I ate, before I talked to any co-workers, I needed to call my parents.

Groaning, I put my head in my hands and leaned forward. I really didn't want to do that, but Lance's words were stuck in my brain, mocking me. I wasn't really prepared. If something bad happened to me, it was up to me to make sure my parents were aware of it.

Reaching into my pocket, I pulled out my phone. The screen was cracked; five months ago, I'd dropped it while walking in the park.

A dog had come racing over to me with its leash trailing from its neck, panting and grinning a big doggy grin, with all of its teeth on display. The owner came stumbling by a few seconds later, but those were a few seconds during which I entertained the possibility I might die from fright.

Pushing the bad memory away, I pulled up my mom's number from my contacts and called her.

The phone rang in my ear three times before Mom picked up. "Martin," she said. "How very nice to hear from you."

"I nearly caught you there, didn't I?" It was a matter of pride for my mother that she never let any phone ring more than four times before answering it. Even if she was in the middle of a meeting, in the bathroom, or already on another call, she was going to answer that phone on time.

"Yes, I was just pulling some cookies out of the oven."

The thought of cookies, fresh-baked and soft, made my stomach growl and my mouth water. Would Lance mind if I baked cookies?

"Is there something you need, Marty, or did you call only for pleasantries?"

We both knew she was beating around the bush to get me to reveal my true intentions on my own, like a true lawyer would. Gritting my teeth, I said, "Neither, actually. I had some news and I thought I should let you know."

"You don't sound like you're about to give me good news."

"That's because I'm not." I was gritting my teeth so hard by this point that I was afraid of cracking a tooth. "There's been a fire. It's right next to my neighborhood."

"A fire in California. Who could have seen that coming?"

"Mom. Please. Your sarcasm is not helping."

"I'm sorry, Marty. It's just that we really did warn you against moving to such a dangerous state. You might as well be living in Florida and wondering where all these hurricanes are coming from."

I winced. She might have been right, in a way. There were fires in California that had been raging for years, fires so intense and strange there were conspiracy theories about them.

However, I didn't think anything like that would ever happen here. Red Bluff was nowhere near the massive forest fires, and we were right next to a river.

There were other reasons I'd moved out here, but those weren't pertinent at the moment. "Everyone in my neighborhood, and the next one over, have to evacuate. It's too close to the fire to be safe to stay."

"I'm so sorry," she said. Her voice finally held some real emotion in it, like she'd only now remembered she was talking to her son. "What are you going to do? Have you evacuated yet?"

"Yeah, I had to as soon as I got home from work." My mother made a soft sound at the mention of work, one which could best be described as a derisive snort. I ignored it, since now wasn't exactly the best time to air out all those old grievances. "I'm staying with a … friend. For the time being."

"What friend is this?"

I groaned. "Mom, I'm 25 years old. I don't have to tell you who I'm hanging around with anymore."

"Be that as it may, it's always best to have as much information as possible in situations like these."

I sighed. It was impossible to lie to my parents. They were lawyers to the core. They had met in college, worked for the same firm before starting up their own. Their lives were rigorous and structured, right down to the nights they had sex.

I was pretty sure they interrogated each other about the experience afterward, too. They knew when someone wasn't telling the truth, which had really made my childhood tough.

"He's a new friend," I said. "A firefighter. His name is Lance."

"Oh, a firefighter? Is he out there fighting *that* fire?"

"Yeah."

"So, you have access to priority information. Well done."

I'm not using him as a fucking witness, Mom. I didn't say anything out loud.

"Well," Mom said, "I'm glad you're safe. I have more to say, but I'm sure your father will say it for me. Here he is."

Before I could protest at being handed over to someone else, I heard the phone being shuffled around. My father cleared his throat, then spoke closer to the phone. "Martin. I've been listening in. I gather there's a fire and you've had to evacuate?"

"Yeah. I'm staying with a friend right now. Just got here."

"Hmm. That's unfortunate. I know how troublesome these acts of God can be."

An act of God, in lawyer terms, had very little to do with an actual God. I didn't really know of any religious lawyers anyway. What the phrase actually referred to was a circumstance caused by nature itself, which a person had no hand in.

"However," my father continued, "I believe that you can handle this to the best of your ability."

My inadequate ability, but he didn't say that out loud.

"Just keep in mind that we're here if you need us. If you have to come home, we'll understand." Dad paused. He continued, softer. "In fact, it might be better for everyone."

"I wouldn't be happy. You know that, Dad."

"You never gave it a chance to make you happy, Martin. Don't give me that kind of talk. You could be a lot more than just another omega who settles down and has his life run by others."

Anger tightened my muscles. I clutched my phone harder until my fingers hurt. "I think I'm going to hang up now, Dad."

"Well, fine, then. Thanks for keeping us updated."

I cut him off before he could say anything else. "Sure, Dad. Love you. Bye."

I hung up and tossed the phone down on the couch, then put my head back in my hands. Now that I no longer had my father's voice in my ear, stirring up my anger, I felt tired and empty.

Having successful lawyers as parents really put a lot of pressure on their only son. Everyone had expected me to turn out like one of them, picking my preferred field of law and running with it. The only problem was that I didn't care about psychology or human nature or figuring out how people ticked so I could pick them apart and manipulate them.

I didn't want to deal with criminals pretending to be innocent, or cause people down on their luck to be pushed deeper into despair. I didn't want intense schooling, long hours, endless paperwork, defensive clients.

I liked animals. No, I loved animals.

Maybe I could have brought my parents some modicum of honor if only I would have become a veterinarian, but I didn't want to see sick and injured pets. That wasn't my interest, either.

What I wanted was to raise them.

I wanted to take care of them all individually, treating them the way they deserved to be treated. I wanted to help each potential owner find the right animal for them, and impart all the knowledge I had on how to properly take care of them. If I could give out that knowledge at the beginning, then there would be that much less need for a vet in the coming years.

I thought of myself kind of like someone who wanted to be a child counselor, addressing issues before they affected lives and turned into much worse problems. Not that it wasn't a good job to be a prison counselor, but that required a different way of thinking. That was dealing with the aftermath.

What I wanted to do was preventative, in a way. From mice, to snakes and tarantulas, to fish, they all deserved a fair chance at the best life possible.

Even dogs. Especially dogs, who were far smarter than they were given credit for. My fear of them didn't stop me from loving them, which was frustrating in all sorts of ways.

It was a personal flaw and it was a career flaw, because I couldn't advance to any higher positions at the store, because those would put me over the grooming, boarding, and adoption sections. I would *have* to work with the dogs, instead of being able to avoid them while stocking and cashiering.

But if I couldn't, then I was going to go nowhere with my life.

The despair dragged at me and I pushed back, trying to straighten up even though every muscle in my body wanted to give up. I wasn't hungry anymore, but I should still eat.

Pushing off the couch, I went into the kitchen and searched through the fridge in search of something bad for me. If this wasn't a day that deserved comfort food, then I didn't know what was.

Chapter 5 - Lance

Before I went back to the fire, I drove Martin's death trap of a car back to the fire department. It was kind of amusing that such a nice, proper guy could stand to drive something like this. Made me wonder how long the *check engine* light had been on. I put it in the parking lot, figuring I could take him here at some point and he could leave again under his own power.

But that wasn't my only reason for being here at the station. I moved inside and started searching through the rooms, whistling and occasionally calling out for who I was searching for. After a minute, I heard faint barking and rapid, eager steps racing down the hallway to my left.

I turned just in time to see twin blurs of black-and-white before the combined one-hundred-pound weight of the dogs slammed into me. I fell back against the wall, laughing a little despite myself, while Spot and Dottie jumped around and nuzzled at my hands, licking me, licking each other.

Their tails wagged with pure joy at the sight of me. If I had a tail myself, it would probably be doing the same thing.

"Spot, Dottie, sit."

There was no need for me to put any sort of command in my voice. Dalmatians were notoriously stubborn and fickle, but I had raised these two from pups. We were a constant feature in each other's lives for going on four years now, and they were so well trained they would obey a baby if the infant's gurgling sounded like a trick they knew.

Spot and Dottie sat instantly, primly, their tails still wagging behind them. Removing one of my gloves, I reached over and stroked their heads, relishing in the softness of their short fur.

Telling them apart was easy for me — for anyone, once the differences were pointed out. They had come from two different litters and I'd picked them out myself, before they even had their markings.

Spot developed into a reject. Breeders and sticklers with fancy tastes looked for Dalmatians with clean, uniform patterns of spots. Spot had large, unsightly patches of black where all of his markings blurred together.

I thought he was unique and beautiful.

Dottie turned out to be a gorgeous queen of a dog, with the desired evenness of spots and pure, clean, unbroken plains of white fur. She had retained a little bit of pinkness underneath her nose, where the fur was so white and fine the skin showed through.

I loved them.

But I wasn't there just for love. These two were working dogs, and they were needed.

I gave them a few more pets, rubbing them behind their ears. "Work time," I said. "Leash. Harness. Go."

Both dogs jumped up and led me to the small closet near where the rest of us got suited up. The dog's supplies were also in there. Food, toys, training treats, leashes and harnesses.

Spot hung back, letting Dottie go first. I hadn't trained him to do that, he'd just decided to be a gentleman on his own. Dottie hopped up onto her hind paws and grabbed a leash in her mouth, then a harness, and brought them over to me. While Spot was doing the same, I put Dottie into her working-dog gear. She puffed out her chest, her head high and proud.

Spot, meanwhile, grinned at me and let his tongue flop out the side of his mouth.

Holding both leashes, I said, "Let's go," and walked out with them to the parking lot. They trotted along, ears up, eyes alert. Their noses quivered, and I wondered if they could smell the smoke from here, if they could sense the danger.

I got the dogs into my truck, threading seatbelts through their harnesses. They stuck their noses out the lowered windows, like any dogs would, sniffing the air as I drove.

Once we arrived back on the scene of the fire, I parked the truck and helped the dogs out. They stood at my feet, ears forward, muscles trembling with eagerness to begin.

The evacuations were still in progress. These two would be invaluable during the process, providing comfort and support for the families, helping to gather everyone together.

They were also trained to detect and respond to a variety of illnesses and injuries. If someone was hurt, had anxiety, epilepsy, heart issues, and something went wrong, we would be alerted and led to them to help them.

Bending down, I took each leash clip in my hand. Spot lifted the fur on his neck for a moment, tickling my fingers.

"Spot. Dottie. Help. Guard."

Two-word commands were all they needed. They knew what to do.

I unclipped their leashes and they raced off, ears flapping and tails streaming out behind them. They kept pace with each other for a few moments, coats brushing together. Then they split away from each other, heading off in different directions. I watched them go, admiring the determination oozing from every centimeter of their bodies.

God, how I loved them.

Too damn bad they weren't mine.

Bitterness curdled at the back of my throat. To distract myself, I also got back to work, relieving someone on the hose. We didn't seem to have made any progress while I was gone, so I focused on doing the best I could to contribute to this primal war.

Even so, I still had Spot and Dottie in the back of my mind. And the letter. That stupid fucking letter.

The Dalmatians were mine to raise and train, with the assistance of a certified working dog trainer, because I had the most experience with dogs. Grew up in the country, spent my entire childhood and all my teen years in the company of terriers, herders, family dogs.

No less than five in the family at a time, and that wasn't counting all the farmhands who brought their dogs to work with them. Mutts, shepherds, huskies. Yeah, I could handle dogs.

But Spot and Dottie didn't belong to me. They were property of the fire department, of Chief Patrick.

I was trying to make them mine, had hired a lawyer to look into ways to do that. The letter had not been positive. Technically, I was fighting for custody.

The only way to win custody was to prove the dogs would be better off living with me full-time. It wasn't an outright failure. It was more of a warning that this would be difficult.

I wasn't going to give up on them. Every time I thought about it, all I had to do was look at them again a little closer and I would get determined.

I hadn't told anyone what I was thinking of yet. The last thing I needed to do was create tension in the place where I worked.

Hours passed. The sky darkened, this time because night had fallen. That didn't really matter too much, since there were lights from the emergency vehicles and even more light coming from the fire itself.

All the same, spotlights were set up, their beams sharp and intense. Even walking in front of one of those things made the temperature rise, and it was hot enough already.

The evacuation ended. The neighborhoods stood empty. Every house was dark and silent, save for the pools of light created by street lamps. No voices, no cars, no sounds of

TV. It was like the end of the world had come to this part of Red Bluff.

Every now and again, a car would approach and be stopped by police, who would explain the danger. The situation was such now that even guided excursions to nearby houses were prohibited. Those unlucky few who arrived home late were turned away with regretful well wishes and reminders to watch the local news for updates. That was after all the yelling stopped, of course.

In the meantime, we kept fighting. Kept working, struggling. Every bit of headway we made was devoured in flames.

We tried drenching the surrounding areas with water to impede the fire, which seemed to work a little. We were all growing tired. Relieving each other and taking turns no longer helped as much as it should have. Short breaks weren't enough to restore us.

Midnight rolled around, and I was given another break. My legs wanted to give out under the sheer weight of my equipment. Instead of dropping down to the ground where I stood, I went back to my truck and picked out some supplies.

"Spot! Dottie!"

The dogs emerged from the smoke, trotting instead of running. Their fur was stained gray with soot.

Wrapping my hands around Spot's face, I rubbed him and stroked him, making low sounds in the back of my throat. He wagged his tail, and Dottie did the same when I petted her.

I gave them both a drink of water, pouring a little bit into their bowl at a time to keep them from drinking too fast and getting sick. I fed them, not enough for a full meal, but enough to give them energy. Then, while they rested, I sat down between them and massaged them, easing the tension from their muscles. I rubbed their legs, their paw pads, their necks.

Dottie rested her head on my leg, and Spot kept smacking me with his paws whenever I tried to rub them. I brought my fists up playfully and pretended to take a swing at his muzzle. He caught my hand in his teeth and shook it, then dropped it and wagged his tail.

A smile rose to my lips and I rubbed his stomach, prompting him to flop over and hike up his leg to expose himself further. Dottie looked on with a mixture of affection and disdain in her big brown eyes. I imagined she was exasperated at how goofy her boyfriend could be.

I could've sat there forever with the two of them wrapped around me. Except I couldn't.

I stood up, and we all got back to work. I thought of the letter, the dogs. And I thought of Martin, with his deep brown eyes and pouty lips.

I had too much to deal with already. I shouldn't have invited him into my home. I was really going to have to be careful with him. I could easily be pulled in by him and give away too much.

Chapter 6 - Martin

After eating dinner, I put a movie in and kept half my attention on it while texting with my co-workers and boss. I also checked the news, local and national. The rest of the world didn't care at all about what was going on in Red Bluff, not that I really expected them to.

However, locally, everyone was talking about the fire. There were already articles being written, and people were being interviewed by members of the press. Our reporters weren't exactly skilled journalists, so those interviews were entertaining more than they were informative.

Everyone had something to say, except there wasn't actually a whole lot being said. There were questions, concerns, theories, and few facts.

Eventually, I gave up and dropped my phone down on the couch beside me. I'd forgotten my charger, and my battery was pretty low at this point. I didn't care. I was tired, wanted to sleep for a thousand years.

I watched the movie, or at least I looked in the general direction of the tv, and eventually I must have fallen asleep because the next thing I knew, I was waking up with a stiff neck. Groaning, I sat up and rubbed at my eyes, which felt sore and sticky. Memories came flooding back to me and I looked around to find that yes, I was still in Lance's house, and he still wasn't home.

I hope he's okay, I thought.

Dinner felt like it had been a long time ago, so I got up and went into the kitchen to make breakfast. Chocolate chip pancakes and sausage. I made extra and stuck the leftovers in the fridge, so Lance could have something to eat when he finally came home.

It wasn't like I was the best cook in the whole world, but I thought that it was the least I could do for him after he had offered me a place to stay. And besides, I wanted to do it. I wanted to do that for him, to have him eat something I had made for him. Why, I wasn't quite sure.

Once breakfast was over, I went to put my dishes in the sink and paused. Indecision raced through me. This wasn't my home. I couldn't just leave this here and expect Lance to clean up after me, when he was out there doing important things.

I'd be a worthless freeloader, taking advantage of him. I wanted him to like me, not hate me.

I want him to like me? Where had that come from?

Shaking my head, I chalked it all up to me being stupid. People usually liked me. They talked to me, told me things as if we'd been friends for years, when in actuality we were strangers who bumped into each other on the street. It was only natural I'd want Lance to like me, when that was what I was used to.

I pushed aside the way he made me feel, the tingling and the flutters and the tension in my groin. Those were all me being stupid.

With my brain cleared, I made a quick decision and went into the living room to gather up all the discarded glasses and other dirty dishes I'd seen last night. Bringing it all back to the kitchen, I ran hot water and added in a generous dose of soap. Then, I got to work, washing dishes, scrubbing, rinsing, drying them off and finding places for them in the cabinets.

I also vacuumed, and swept, and tidied up the counters. The busywork relaxed me, and I even found myself starting to hum a little bit.

Then the front door opened. A deep, gruff voice called out into the house. "You didn't leave this unlocked all night, did you?"

My cheeks burned. I set down the rag I'd been using to wipe off the stovetop and went into the living room. "Maybe?" I said, hesitantly.

Lance stood in the foyer, filling the open doorway with his broad shoulders. His hair was flattened, but sticking up in ruffles at the back. The color was dark brown, like I'd thought, with some rich red hints where the sunlight hit.

The sight of him would have taken my breath away if it wasn't for the way he looked so dead tired, like he was about to fall asleep on his feet. He looked like only a ghost of the powerful hero who'd rescued me from homelessness.

"What if someone decided to rob the place?" he grunted. "You'd be in danger."

His voice was so guttural I felt it resonate in my chest, like the beat of a drum. "I think if someone was going to break into houses tonight, they'd go to all those abandoned ones near the fire. They're all just sitting empty. Mine included."

"Heh." He actually said the word like that, speaking his laughter. "You got a point. Just be more careful. I didn't save you only for you to get killed, you know."

I nodded and swallowed hard. I noticed he was keeping the front door open, even though he had already taken off his socks and shoes. Weird.

"You vacuum?" He fixed me with his blue-green gaze. It was hard to breathe when he did that, but I also couldn't look away. My stomach tingled.

"Yes. I cleaned. I hope you don't mind. I just thought you might like to come home to a clean house."

"You saying my house is dirty?"

"No! I just didn't want to add to the mess. Not that there was a mess. I mean. Um."

I was really, really fucking this up. I wished I could sink down into the floor and disappear.

Lance made another of those spoken-laugh sounds. His eyes sparkled, showing the real depth of his amusement. "Relax, okay? I'm just fucking with you. After the night I've had, I could use a little joking around."

I hadn't taken that into account. I nodded and rubbed the back of my neck, trying to get my heart to stop beating so fast. "I made breakfast. There's leftovers in the fridge, if you want them."

Lance nodded slowly, his lips curving in a tired way that made me feel as if my brain was spinning inside my skull. "I thought I smelled something. Chocolate?"

I found myself smiling back at him. "You've got a good nose." It was an awkward compliment, but it worked because his lips curved higher. "Chocolate chip pancakes."

"Can't go wrong with that. Thanks for not eating all of them." He winked, showing me he was teasing again, then turned his head and let out a whistle in the direction of the open door.

What?

Suspicion blossomed like a time lapse of flowers, spreading sharp petals across my mind. I started to back away, but it was too late, they were already inside, rushing at me, pinning me with their eyes.

Two massive dogs. Dalmatians. They bounced around me, touching me, pushing in on my space, leaving streaks of dirt and filthy paw prints everywhere they went.

Panic climbed high in my throat, and all the blood drained from my face. Before I could control myself, before I could do anything at all, I let out a shriek that would have been more at home coming from the throat of a six-year-old girl.

"Spot! Dottie! Get back here!"

Through the film of gray terror clouding my vision, I watched as the dogs stopped in their tracks and went over to sit calmly at Lance's feet, like lions at the side of an emperor. My heart hammered in my throat and I put my hand to my head, feeling the beginnings of a stress headache forming rapidly.

Lance looked at the dogs in a casual manner. "Stay."

Tails wagged. The dogs stayed. They looked much smaller now that they weren't throwing themselves at me, about the size that Dalmatians should be. Except he'd called one Dottie, and that was a female name, but they both looked male-sized to me.

I wasn't even making sense to myself anymore.

Lance came over to me and placed his hand on my shoulder, gripping me. I latched onto the sensation and tried to breathe calmer, to no avail. I was still gasping, still a little unhinged, on the verge of a panic attack.

"You're afraid of them, or did they startle you?" he asked, voice low.

"Both," I managed.

"Right. Well." His eyes were greener now than they had been, slightly darker than before. The change in color captivated me, and I pulled in a deeper breath without being aware of it.

"Spot and Dottie are firefighter dogs. They live part-time with me for relaxation and recovery. They might be big, but they won't hurt you. They only wanted to see who was here, since no one else usually is."

"It's not them," I said, admitting it. Admitting a terrible secret to a man I hardly knew, for a reason I didn't understand. "All dogs. It's all dogs."

Lance leaned back from me, taking his hand away and letting it drop down by his side. His jaw tightened, and he looked back over at the two dogs.

If he had to choose between the dogs and letting me stay here, I knew exactly which one it would be. If I was in the same situation, no way in hell would I have chosen me. I prepared for rejection, for disappointment, squaring my shoulders.

Lance placed his hand on my shoulder again, startling me. His touch was gentler, and it sparked something inside me that I probably shouldn't have been feeling right then.

"Don't worry about it, okay?" Lance said. "I'm going to eat. I'm going to feed my dogs. Then, we're all going to take a nap. When I wake up, I've got two filthy dogs to wash. We'll talk after that."

"You aren't going to make me leave?" I whispered.

Lance's eyes widened the slightest bit. He looked me up and down, and I felt as if he was seeing more than just my appearance, like he was looking into my soul. The whole thing was strangely intimate, and my stomach started to tingle again, way deep down inside me.

"No. I am not going to make you leave. I said you could stay here, and that hasn't changed. I can't kick out someone like you, anyway."

Someone like me. He probably meant a pitiful omega with no resources, no skills to speak of. The world would eat me alive if I was left to my own devices, that was for sure.

"Let me go and get the dog food from the kitchen. I'll feed them in my room." Lance stepped away.

I grabbed his arm without thinking. My hands couldn't have wrapped all the way around his muscles even if I'd put them both together into a circle. His skin was smooth and soft, stretched taut over the rolling hill of his biceps.

This firefighter was about to start a fire inside me, the sensations inside me overriding even my fear. "Wait! What if they... move?"

"They do anything, you tell them to sit. They'll listen." Lance suddenly let out a chuckle, a real laugh. I hadn't managed to get that out of him, but his dogs could. "Take them out to a dog park, and they obey commands they hear way over on the other side. You'll be fine. Trust me."

With one hand, he removed mine from his arm. He held my fingers for a moment or two longer, then moved away in the direction of the kitchen. I could still feel his touch on me.

And I could feel the dogs watching me. I turned my head to look at them, saw them studying me with their big brown eyes. I caught sight of something telling on one of them and figured that the other must be Dottie. Even knowing she was a female, I still couldn't have identified her as female on sight.

I looked away again, feeling my heart start to pound again just from focusing on them.

Lance came back, toting along two metal dog bowls and a container of kibble. "Come," he said, still as casually as if he were talking to a human. The dogs hopped up and trotted eagerly after him, close enough to tromp on his heels several times before they all disappeared into the bedroom. A metallic cascading sound told me that food was being poured into bowls.

Lance reappeared a few moments later, carrying the food container. He headed for the kitchen and I followed this time, lingering in the doorway to see where he put the food. It went into the only cupboard I hadn't opened, which was why I hadn't seen it and had had no warning about the dogs.

I could be a pretty awkward person at times, but no amount of weirdness I'd ever experienced before could hold a candle to watching Lance wander around his kitchen, reheating breakfast leftovers. In the silence between us, I was acutely aware of the background sounds of the house. The air conditioning and the fridge hummed to each other, and the ceiling fan over the dining room table let out measured clicks as it spun in circles. The clock on the wall ticked.

After only a minute, I felt like I might go out of my mind if I had to listen to all these damnable metronomes any longer. Lance sat at the table, eating mechanically, and I couldn't tell whether he thought my cooking was good or not. The uncertainty and the ticking, the clicking, nagged at me and I could deal with it no longer. I blurted out the first thing that came into my mind. "Dottie is pretty big for a girl."

Lance chewed, swallowed. I watched the motion of his lips and throat, a shiver running down my spine. He set his fork down on his half-empty plate and looked up at me with a sigh.

"All right. You've got me, Martin. Let's have that conversation now, not later. Take a seat."

I sat down next to him and waited while he studied his hands, seeming to search for something to say. "You're afraid of dogs. Why?"

He had every right to ask that of me, so I had to answer. "I was bitten by one when I was younger. Look."

I held out my arm and turned slightly, pointing at some mottled markings on my skin. They were old scars, pale white, and a lot of people mistook them as birthmarks when they first saw them.

"I was five, I think. We had a neighbor with a dog that no one would ever go near. I thought it was lonely. One day I found myself alone and unwatched, so I crawled under a gap beneath the fence and went to the dog house to try and pet the dog."

"Shit," Lance swore. "What kind of dog?"

"A mix. I'm not sure." I shrugged. "My neighbor was in the yard gardening, with his back turned. If he hadn't been there, I probably would have gotten my throat torn out.

"I still had to go to the hospital. I needed dozens of stitches. That dog grabbed onto me and it shook me. I remember my neighbor telling my parents that I was being thrown around in the air like a chew toy."

I didn't have much of a recollection of the event, myself. My long-term memory wasn't the best, so most of my childhood years were blurs punctuated with photographic moments of clarity. Still, thinking of that time made my stomach turn and the old scars on my arm ached with phantom pain, like I'd been bitten all over again. Dread hovered over me like a cloud.

"It was an abused dog?" Lance asked, his voice hushed. He had stopped eating entirely. Having his full attention on me made me feel shy and very aware of myself.

"Yes, but, like, not in the way you're thinking." I shook my head. "It was all a terrible accident. I've heard the full story tons of times, growing up.

"That neighbor, he adopted the dog from a kill shelter. It was on death row. No one wanted it because it was so aggressive. He was trying to work with it, and everyone in the neighborhood was just respecting his request to give it some space and leave it alone.

"I got in that dog's face and it was scared, so it attacked. I know all that. I don't blame it. The cops didn't get involved, and nothing happened."

"What happened with the dog afterwards?"

"I don't know," I said. "We moved a few years later for something unrelated. A job opportunity for my parents." I clenched my hands into fists. "I don't hate dogs, Lance. I don't want you to get the wrong idea."

"But you're still afraid of them after all this time." Lance pushed his hand back through his hair. A puff of soot rose up and then settled down around his shoulders. "You know most dogs aren't aggressive, don't you?"

"I know that! I love all kinds of animals. I even handle spiders and cockroaches at the store where I work.

"I think dogs are great. I wish I could pet them. I wish … but every time I get too close to one, something deep inside me kicks in and makes me afraid. It's instinct, I guess. I can't control it."

Lance gave me a puzzled look. "Where do you work, that there are spiders and cockroaches?"

"Hissing cockroaches," I said. "They're pets."

"You work at a pet store."

"I work at Pet Central, yes."

Lance held up his hand, making a back-up gesture. "That's a dog-friendly environment. I've even taken Spot and

Dottie in there myself. How the hell do you work like that? How did you get hired?"

Guilt scurried up my spine, and I turned my head away. "They don't ask if you're scared of dogs during the interview," I muttered.

Lance let out a startled laugh and shook his head slowly. "You have guts, Martin. I'm impressed. You must really, really love animals if you're willing to work in an environment that makes you constantly afraid."

Having this hero be impressed by me made me blush. Grinning, I said, "You're impressive too. You must really like fires."

My joke fell flat. Lance curled his lip and straightened up, pushing away from the table. He scraped the rest of his breakfast into the trash, then set the plate in the sink.

I didn't know what I had said to set him off and I didn't actually get a chance to find out, because I was distracted when he bent over. The full, firm shape of his ass pushed against his pants. I could see the way the material folded between his cheeks, creating a teasing divot. My mouth went dry.

Lance turned around, his gaze meeting mine. He leaned over the table and looked into my face, eyelids lowered. "Like what you see?"

I couldn't speak. It felt like any words that came out of my mouth would be the wrong ones. I couldn't even move.

I just waited and hoped that Lance would make a move, prayed that he wouldn't, two parts of me fighting over what I wanted more. I was a nobody. I could be attracted to him, but there was no way he would ever be attracted back to me.

Lance made a small sound, like a growl. His breath hit my lips, hot and sweet. I could almost taste the chocolate on his lips, sticky-sweet pancake syrup.

Then he leaned back and straightened up. His eyes were dark, and I couldn't tell what he might be thinking. "Okay."

That was it. Just "okay," which really didn't mean anything at all.

I scrambled for something to say and brought out the first thing in my head. "So, you're going to let me stay here?"

He nodded slowly. I hoped he didn't mind that I'd changed the subject. "Yeah, I am. Of course I am. You don't have anywhere else to go, so I can't make you leave.

"The only problem is going to be with the dogs, but they'll be off working with me most of the day. When we're home, I'll make sure they don't bother you. Is that good enough?"

"I feel bad about making you make allowances for me."

Lance smiled a little. "That's okay. Being in this job kind of gives you a new perspective on things. Sure, I'd prefer not to be woken up in the middle of the night, but if it's for the greater good, then I'll do it. No use being annoyed by something I signed up for."

So that was it. He had signed up for this. I didn't really mean anything to him. He might not even really be attracted to me; he was just making the best of the situation.

I'd make the best of it too, then. I just hoped I could.

This mishap with the dogs made me worry about worse

problems somewhere down the line.

Chapter 7 - Lance

A week had passed since that fateful day when the fire blazed out of control. The situation did not improve at all. The flames quickly claimed the rest of the fairgrounds and crept into the surrounding areas, edging in on yards. All of us were doing the best we could, around the clock, and it wasn't good enough.

I drifted around in a cloud of despair and dread no matter where I was or what I was doing. Things had gone terribly wrong, I was responsible, and I could not fix the result.

The knowledge weighed so heavily on me that the other firefighters I worked with were starting to notice the difference, asking me what was wrong or if I was sick. Shep even dared suggest I take a break, as if the department could afford to lose even one fighter right about now.

I snapped at him, and everyone else, warning them to mind their own business. They all left me alone, though I saw them giving me sideways glances sometimes when they didn't think I was watching.

Whatever. I didn't care about their companionship, not really. We were brothers in arms, comrades, united towards a single goal. That didn't make us friends, so let them think whatever they wanted, as long as they weren't suspicious of me.

The only thing I did care about was the dogs. They sensed my weakening resolve and it affected their confidence, making them doubt themselves. I couldn't properly care for them at home, when Martin was there, so I spent long hours at the station pampering them.

I fed them treats and played endless games of fetch to boost their spirits. Really, being around Spot and Dottie was the only time I felt complete and okay anymore. Some part of me had come unhinged at the start of all this and was hanging loose, threatening to fall away.

I didn't know what would happen after that.

Maybe I would have been okay if I only had the fire to deal with, but that wasn't the case. Martin. It would have been wrong to call him an obstacle. He was more like a new feature, one I hadn't gotten used to yet.

He had nowhere to go, and the house wasn't all that big. It was only common sense that we would constantly be around each other. It got to be where I felt his presence so acutely, could feel him coming down the hall even when I couldn't see or hear him. He occupied a space which had previously been empty, causing the household to revolve around him like a wayward sun.

The worst part was that it wasn't all bad. Actually, it wasn't bad at all. He kept meals in the fridge for me and kept me company while I ate, occasionally asking the usual get-to-know-you questions.

How long had I lived in Red Bluff? When did I decide I wanted to be a firefighter? What other jobs had I had?

And when I didn't want to talk, he gave me my peace and silence without question. That felt good, too.

Plus, he was nice to look at. I kept catching myself observing him, making my groin tighten with the beginnings of desire.

With my thoughts confused and swirling around inside my head, I entered the fire station with Spot and Dottie struggling to keep pace. Their heads hung low and their tails were limp. They were exhausted, and so was I.

I had just finished a 48-hour on-call session, and now had the next 24 hours to rest and recuperate before jumping back into the fray. All I wanted was to go home and sleep forever.

Rubbing my eyes, I staggered through the desolate hallways of the station until I reached the equipment room. Spot and Dottie lounged on the floor by the entrance while I stripped off my gear and pulled on my normal clothes, which felt too light and too loose after all this time. My stomach growled, and I wondered idly what Martin had made for dinner last night.

The casual nature of my own thoughts was a little startling. It was almost like we were roommates.

Or a couple.

"Come on, you two," I said, focusing on the dogs to avoid following that train of thought. The dogs came over to me and I picked up their leashes to walk them outside to the truck. After getting them harnessed up, I hopped behind the wheel and drove home.

Something happened as I drove, something I had been aware of for the past several days but hadn't yet been able to figure out. The closer I got to home, the more my spirits rose.

I felt lighter, almost relieved. My shoulders relaxed, and I breathed a little easier. It couldn't be just because I was going home, since this was a new feeling to me. Something had changed.

By the time I pulled into the driveway, I had come no closer to a conclusion about these strange feelings inside me. Shrugging, I decided not to question it. Feeling good was better than feeling like I'd been crushed flat by a steamroller.

Even Spot and Dottie seemed to be feeling the difference. Tired as they were, they managed to walk with a bit of pep in their step, and their ears perked up.

"Feels good to be home, doesn't it?" I said to them, and opened the front door. The three of us piled inside and I shut the door, bending over to get their leashes off.

As soon as I touched Spot, I sensed his tension. His muscles were firm underneath his fur, his posture stiff. Puzzled, I looked up and saw Martin standing in the middle of the living room with the vacuum cleaner held in one hand. He fluttered his fingers at me, his voice soft and shy and sweet. "Welcome home, Lance. And Lance's dogs."

I looked back down at Spot. He held his ears forward in Martin's direction, his nose quivering. Next to him, Dottie was doing the same thing. She made a soft sound in the back of her throat, which could have been mistaken for a growl by someone who hadn't spent a lot of time with dogs. It was a curious sound, a questioning chuff. She was asking something. Both of them were.

I glanced over at Martin again, who had given up on us and was busily winding up the vacuum cord. Watching him perform such a domestic task caused my heart to twist inside my chest.

This was what was different. We weren't only coming home. We were coming home to Martin, the newest fixture in our lives. The dogs liked him, wanted to make friends, wondered if today would be the day he finally accepted them.

As for myself, maybe it was the same thing. As much as he disrupted things, here I was, excited about coming home to him. He always had a smile ready for me, always looked at me as though everything I had to say was important to him.

He held conversations well, even if he listened more than he talked. His occasional awkwardness was endearing, making him seem far more genuine than those people who always knew exactly what to say.

I liked his little stumbles, his stammers, his blushes.

Hell, I liked it when he asked me about my day. It was a bullshit question, the kind most people didn't actually want answered. The difference was that Martin cared. He wanted to know.

It felt good to talk to someone about what I had gone through during the day, especially someone who could look at the situation with fresh eyes. Try talking to a firefighter about fighting a fire and he would tell you to knock it off; he was relaxing and didn't want to hear about that shit.

I am in over my head, I thought.

Martin crossed the living room to get to the closet, still giving the dogs a wide berth. "How was your day?" he asked, that magical question.

"Long, stressful," I said. The same shit I always said. I hesitated, thought about leaving it there, and gave in. He did so much for me; he deserved more. "If this goes on much longer, we'll start losing houses. You think the smoke is bad now, wait until a house goes up. Everyone will be wearing masks."

"I saw some people wearing masks earlier today," Martin said. He looked tentative, and I motioned for him to continue. "This must be awful for people with asthma or allergies."

"Yeah. I bet it is." Struggling with my guilt, I took the dogs back to my bedroom and fed them their food, then petted them until they grew tired. I still kept petting them, reluctant to leave.

Each motion of my hand passing through their fur sent up puffs of gray soot, leaving clean tracks behind. They smelled more like fire than animal, which sucked a bit. I'd always liked the smell of dogs. Nothing else like it, so clean and alive and free.

Spot snuffled and rested his head on my thigh. I rubbed his ear, and he made a quiet groan of pleasure. In response, Dottie whined. She wanted both of us to shut up and stop moving so she could sleep.

Holding back my chuckle, I gave them both a last pat, relishing in the softness of their fur. I pushed myself to my feet and went to the bedroom door, then lingered there, watching them.

Dottie shifted, snuggling herself closer to Spot, who draped a paw over her flank. They were the picture of trust and contentment, the sight of them enough to bring tears to my eyes.

Burning, stinging tears, and a tickle in my sinuses. I suddenly felt my tiredness much more acutely, and staggered out into the hallway in search of something to eat before I passed out.

Martin was in the kitchen, standing there waiting for me, as usual. I wanted to stop and appreciate the sight of him, but I forced myself to keep moving. He didn't always seem to like it when I looked at him for too long, which sometimes made me wonder if I was reading his signals correctly.

"Hey," I said, heading past him to the fridge.

"How are the dogs?" Martin asked. He came up very close to my shoulder while talking, our bodies almost touching. If I twitched, we would bump together. "They looked a little ragged to me."

I pulled out Tupperware containers, which were neatly labeled with the contents and dates, searching for the most recent one. "They're working their asses off, like the rest of us. Once they've slept, I'll feed them something special. Maybe steak."

"I can cook a steak while you're sleeping," Martin said, his voice shy. I looked over at him while tucking the containers

I didn't want back on the shelves. "I don't really like steak, but I don't think the dogs will be too picky if I cook it badly."

"You don't like steak? What red-blooded American man doesn't like steak?" I stared at Martin, pinning him with my gaze. He wore a fitted red t-shirt and skinny jeans, which left very little to the imagination.

He turned his head, trying to hide his blush behind the curls of his hair. "Meat is good for you," I said. "It builds muscle."

"I like meat," Martin murmured. "Just not steak. Too tough."

I went over to the microwave and stuck the container inside, jabbing at the buttons. Something rose inside me and I couldn't control myself. I turned around and moved closer to Martin, pressing into his space until we were nearly touching again.

He stared up at me, looking like his eyes might pop out of his head. His body trembled, and his apparent uncertainty might have made me back off if I hadn't noticed the way he shifted his legs, his rapid breathing.

I took the chance and leaned in even closer to him, letting my body do as it wanted. I needed to be closer, to feel his body on mine.

"What kind of meat do you like?"

His lips parted. No words came out. I felt his breath and licked my lips. My groin throbbed for him, and images of what I might do to him flashed through my brain. I pictured him underneath me in a variety of positions, imagined how he would feel with his muscles taut and his skin slick with sweat.

I wanted him. I deserved a break, after all this hell I'd gone through, and I was going to have him.

Grabbing his chin in my hand, I felt delicate stubble pushing through his skin. He stared up at me, eyes shimmering. Then he closed his eyes and pursed his perfect pouting lips.

I brought my lips to his and kissed him, claiming his lips with mine. He was so soft, and he tasted so sweet. Pressing my mouth harder on his, I teased him with my tongue, causing his lips to part. I slid my tongue between, tasting him more clearly.

His mouth was hot and wet, and when his tongue flicked out to meet mine, I thought I might soar away from how good it felt. My pants were suddenly tight and painful as my cock came to attention, straining in Martin's direction. I pushed him, forcing him back against the counter.

Need surged high and bright behind my flickering eyelids. I clutched at Martin's hips, dropped my hands to the front of his jeans and tugged at his zipper. I was shaking, almost overcome with the urge to take him. All of the back-and-forth between us, the sly looks, the awkwardness, the hints, it was culminating in this. I was going to…

A hand on my chest pushed me away.

I reared back like a startled stallion, torn out of my fervor by the rejection. It stung a lot more than it should have to be told no by him.

Martin bit his lip. I moved my thumb to rescue his soft, pouting lip from the snare of his teeth, but he went right back to it.

I wished he would stop. My body was getting mixed signals from him. No was no, but he looked so irresistible…

"You want this," I told him. My chest was tight, my voice constricted into a deep growl. "Don't tell me you don't want this. The way you look at me. The way you act."

"I…"

I didn't give him a chance. I pressed on. "I can feel your dick. You're horny. Let me help with that."

"I want to!" The exclamation seemed to burst from him. He looked mortified, his face pink. "I want to, Lance. I don't know if this is the right time, though."

It took a whole lot of effort to peel myself away from him. I didn't want to, but I would respect his boundaries.

"Fine. Whatever you want. You let me know when you think it's time. Don't wait too long, though. We're going to try some new tactics with the fire. You might be able to go home soon."

"Oh. Okay, sure. It would be nice to go home." He looked and sounded surprised that I'd given up so easily.

I shrugged again, this time mentally. I wasn't going to waste my time with something that wasn't going to happen.

As much as I liked Martin, as much as I would have enjoyed fucking him, there were various warning signs which told me not to spend too much effort on him. We weren't going to work out, long-term.

That's what I said to myself. Why didn't I believe it? Why did I want to take a step back and reevaluate things?

The silence between us turned awkward. Martin slithered away from the counter without touching me. He moved over to the dining room table, picking up a drinking glass. The glass sweated with condensation, droplets of water trickling over the back of his hand.

I took my dinner out of the microwave. It was still steaming hot, which surprised me. So many things had happened in a very short amount of time.

I dug around in my silverware drawer, searching for a fork that wasn't too badly bent. Maybe it was time to invest in some more expensive utensils. That, or give up and switch to plastic.

"Dottie really *is* a big girl dog, isn't she?"

I looked over at Martin, not really surprised that he was already trying to start up the conversation again. I was glad he had, whether I'd tell him that or not.

"You asked that question before."

"Well, I never got an answer."

I leaned my hip on the counter, shoveling too-hot food into my mouth. "Yes, she is. She's the perfect Dalmatian. Big and beautiful and smart."

"You must be really happy to have her. And Spot, too. Are they brother and sister?"

"Heh. They might as well be, the way they've grown up together."

I shrugged, shoved more food into my mouth. Now that I'd started eating, my hunger had heightened in intensity. I wanted to be able to satisfy at least one of my needs. "But, no. They aren't from the same litter."

"You trained them yourself?"

"Yeah, I did. With some help." I didn't want to talk about this. "Find a different subject, Martin. Please."

He looked away. "Maybe we should just stop here. So you can finish eating and get some rest. I won't bother you again."

Martin moved away, heading into the living room. He had been sleeping on my couch over the course of this past week, and he had set up quite the little nest in there, surrounding himself with all of his things.

I finished my dinner and put my plate in the sink. Tiredness was making me do weird things. I really needed sleep.

I crossed back through the living room, very aware of every move I made and the way Martin kept throwing glances at me. I went into my bedroom, shutting the door behind me. Turning around, I saw that Spot and Dottie had vacated their spot on the floor and were both curled up on my bed.

Chuckling, I climbed into bed and lay down on my back with a dog on either side. They automatically moved to make room for me, their bodies warm and comforting against mine.

"You guys have it easy," I murmured.

Spot made a snuffling sound to tell me he was listening.

"You don't know how easy you have it. You're just dogs. You eat and sleep and shit and work. I take care of you. You don't have to worry about anything else."

I often talked to them like this. They paid attention whenever I did. I knew they were trying to figure out what I was saying, that they couldn't actually understand, but it felt nice to get some things out in the open on occasion.

Felt nice to have someone talk back, too. That was something Martin could give me that the dogs couldn't.

I pushed that thought away. I stroked Dottie, who was snoring and twitching in her sleep. "You don't have to worry about having secrets or regrets. You don't have to worry about people coming in and out of your life."

I sighed. "I wish I had someone to do that for me. It'd make everything so much easier. I'm so confused, guys."

Spot licked my hands. I couldn't tell if it was a genuine show of support because he sensed my emotions, or if he was tasting my dinner. Probably the latter, because he was Spot. A goofball.

My goofball, someday.

"There are so many different things going on right now. It's all so stressful. I don't know if I have what it takes to handle it all. I'm..."

The rest of the words wouldn't come. I couldn't bring myself to say them out loud.

I'm ashamed.

This was all completely and utterly my fault. The good feelings and the bad, they all arose from the fire.

The fire that I had caused.

The fire I had set up so carefully, which had somehow gone wildly out of control. Everything was at risk because of me. Homes, lives. If anyone ever found out about this, I was ruined.

Whatever was going on between me and Martin would fall apart before we had a chance to decide if it was something to pursue. I would lose the dogs.

I was such a fuck-up.

I lay there on my back, staring up at the ceiling, waiting for sleep to come claim me. My heart pounded wildly in my chest and my thoughts raced, defying my physical exhaustion.

Sleep, I told myself. I closed my eyes and forced myself to hold still, fighting against the restlessness and impatience crawling up my spine.

My limbs grew heavy and somehow, eventually, I drifted away.

Chapter 8 - Martin

I touched my lips for the umpteenth time, feeling a sense of wonder rise in me again. I had never been kissed like that before, so wildly and sweetly all at once. It had made me feel out of control, like some more primal part of me was rising to the surface.

My dick had been so on-board with the pleasure, begging for more. I had felt like I might die if I didn't get some attention down there.

And then I'd gone and messed it all up by pushing Lance away. I'd had this sudden moment of clarity that shone through the haze of need, flashing in my eyes and reminding me that I wasn't worth much of anything at all.

Unsuccessful, fearful. What would a guy like Lance possibly want with someone like me? It was just convenient for him, that was all. I was a good target for him, and he'd honed in on me.

A lot of people did that. They knew I'd give them the time of day when no one else would, so they talked to me, spilled their secrets, shared things they probably shouldn't. This was no different.

It *felt* different, but I was probably lying to myself.

Sighing, I reached for the book I'd started reading earlier and held it up in front of my face. I couldn't concentrate, and the words swam around in front of my eyes, so it took me a lot longer than it should have for me to realize that I was holding it upside down. Frustrated, I tossed the book down on the couch beside me and reached for the TV remote on the coffee table.

I aimed at the remote at the screen and went to push the power button, to fill my mind with endless, meaningless, mind-numbing chatter.

A voice disturbed the stillness before I had even pushed the button.

I paused, listening hard. The voice was low, rising in and out of audibility. Lance was talking, but to whom? There was no one in the house except him and myself.

And the dogs. Could he be talking to the dogs?

Maybe he's giving them a pep talk, I thought, and stifled a giggle. *Or reading them a bedtime story.*

Either way, I was intrigued. Standing up, I crept across the living room and down the short hall. My every movement seemed abnormally loud in the stillness, and I half expected Lance to jump out at me at any moment.

When I stood outside Lance's doorway, my heartbeat throbbed so intensely in my ears that I could hardly make out what he was saying. Still, even when I missed a word here and there, I got the gist of what he was saying.

He was lonely. He wanted someone to be there for him. To help him.

Part of me thought that didn't make much sense. He had an entire network of people who would support him. He was a firefighter. Other firefighters should be there for him, plus anyone else who was in uniform.

I wouldn't have been surprised if a random person on the street would gladly listen to him once they found out who he was. His position demanded respect.

Demanded.

Maybe that was it. He wanted something that didn't have to do with his job. Something that happened naturally, and wasn't forced.

I bit my lip as an idea started to form.

The attraction between us was pretty natural. We hadn't really talked about it. It had just kind of happened, and had escalated into that kiss in the kitchen.

If I'd let Lance turn that kiss into something more intense, he wouldn't be having this conversation with the dogs. I'd had a chance to satisfy him, and I'd blown it.

Next time, I wouldn't stop him.

I was already taking up time and resources from him. I should give something back to him to make up for it. I'd make myself useful by helping him to relax. Personally, I always felt relaxed after I'd blown off some steam, so Lance should be the same way.

I stepped away from his bedroom door. If the dogs hadn't been in there, I'd have barged in and finished what we started. As it was, I would have to bide my time and wait for my chance.

Lance spent most of that day and night resting, recovering his strength. He only emerged from his bedroom to eat. I was ready for him, but not because I'd cooked.

Instead, I waved a $20 at him. "You want pizza tonight?"

Lance studied me. "Is this bribery?"

"Like you would take a bribe?"

"I would if it's pizza. I don't care what you get, as long as it's unhealthy."

I smiled and placed an order for a large four-meat pizza, which was due to arrive in half an hour. Until then, I had to find something to talk about that wouldn't be extremely awkward.

"What do you do for fun?"

Lance glanced over at me. "Fun?"

"You have to have fun sometime, right? Things can't always be this busy for you."

"Yeah, you're right." He stared down at his hands, thinking. "Mostly, I spend time with Spot and Dottie. Or I join some of the other off-duty firefighters for dinner and drinks. We play cards a lot. I am an undefeated War champion."

"Isn't War a game of chance?"

"Not when you know how to control the shuffle." He grinned and shrugged. "And maybe sometimes I've got high number cards from another deck shoved up my sleeve."

I laughed. "I didn't take you for a cheater!"

"It's not cheating if no one's made any rules yet." Silence fell for a heartbeat or two. "What do you do for fun, Martin?"

"I like to go to the overlook at the river," I said.

"Pretty romantic. I bet you don't go there alone."

I blushed and rubbed the back of my neck. "You might want to stick to betting on games of War. I don't bring guys with me or anything like that. I just like to be alone. It's peaceful. Even more when I've had a beer or two."

"What's your poison?"

"Whatever the special is at the Red Bluff Inn. That's my favorite bar. Do you know it?" I asked.

"Yeah. I usually go to the Pine Tavern, myself. It's a bit more redneck. Speaks to the country boy in me."

"Country boy?" I remembered trying to ask about his past before, and getting no real answers. He wouldn't even say how long he'd lived in Red Bluff.

"What else do you do?" he asked, clearly evading the question again.

"I like to go for walks around the parks," I said, racking my brain. Being so close to him always made it a little difficult to think. "And I like to go to Walmart, especially when it's late and all the interesting night owls come out. And when it's ice cream season, I stop by the parlor on the way home from work basically every day."

"Hm."

That was all he said, like his enthusiasm for the conversation had died. I sat back deeper against the couch, disappointed, but elated all the same. Every bit I found out about him only made me more interested in him. He was an enigma.

It was hard to imagine Lance as a good old country boy, a farmer's kid who was destined to grow up, marry a high school sweetheart, have babies with them, and take over the family business.

Then again, I couldn't picture myself as a slick city lawyer. Maybe displacement from our youths was something he and I had in common.

The pizza arrived and we ate, mostly in silence. He thanked me, then retreated to his bedroom.

The next day, he went to the fire station for another 48-hour shift. In his absence, I planned. I rehearsed. I waited. As time drew nearer, each passing hour left me feeling more and more impatient. I'd committed myself to this, and now I wanted to follow through with it.

On the morning that Lance was due to return home, I busied myself with baking some muffins. I could cook just fine, but I'd never had much success with baking. I wanted this to be an extra-special gesture.

The scents of cinnamon and sugar clung to me like a perfume. I had to smile. This gave a whole new meaning to "looked good enough to eat." I'd be dessert.

Just as I pulled the muffins out of the oven and set them aside to cool, I heard the front door open. I hurried over to watch Lance come inside. He shut the door behind himself and kicked off his boots.

Something seemed different, and I immediately figured out what it was. Fear pierced through me like a sewing needle. "Where's Spot and Dottie? Are they okay?"

"Yeah," Lance said. "I left them at the station. Sucks, but they're needed there."

"Why is that? Is something going on?"

Please answer. Please tell me what's on your mind.

If Lance thought I was being pushy, he didn't give any sign of it. In fact, he seemed eager to talk. "They're going to try a new tactic with the fire. It might get tense, and they want the dogs there to watch for danger.

"They notice it faster than the rest of us do, even though we've been at it twice as long." He sounded admiring. I couldn't help but to smile at the idea that he looked up to his dogs.

"I made muffins, if you want to try some. I've got coffee brewing, too. If you want to talk about the new tactic, or anything. You know I'll listen."

Lance nodded and patted my shoulder. "Thanks."

He moved past me and our hips brushed together, either on purpose or by accident. No matter which one it was, it took my breath away. I followed after him and fetched a coffee cup for him. "How do you like it?"

"I can get my own coffee," he said.

Disappointed, I handed over the cup and watched while he fixed his own breakfast, piling muffins onto a plate. The muffins still steamed, perfuming the air with cinnamon. They looked perfect, if a little plain. I should have put some crumble on top to make them look better.

Lance sat at the table, momentarily ignoring his food in favor of his coffee. He slugged down the entire mug's worth in only a few long swallows, then let out a breathy sound of appreciation. A few drops of coffee clung to his lips and his tongue flicked out, swiping them away.

I trembled a little on the inside, imagining his tongue doing similar things to me. Memories of when we had kissed rose high inside me, and I touched my lips absentmindedly, remembering the way he had claimed me. My lips had felt tender afterward.

"You're acting weird, Martin."

I must have been really transparent if he could tell that. All the same, I tried not to show that he was right. "What do you mean?"

"Muffins? Wanting to make my coffee for me? You're being very accommodating. More than usual."

I rubbed the back of my neck and looked away. "I want to help you."

Lance narrowed his eyes. The look was somehow sexual, and I felt a thrill pulse through my body. Maybe I was getting ahead of myself. "Help me?"

"Look," I said. I came over to the table and put my hands down on the top, watching Lance through a veil of hot air. "I overheard you in the bedroom the other day."

"You what?" Lance leaned back, his turquoise eyes darkening, his expression guarded. I thought he might be trying to remember what all he'd said that I might have heard. I'd only come in for the last part of his talk with the dogs, so I didn't know what I might have missed. "You eavesdropped, is what you did."

I blushed. "Well, I heard you talking, and I wanted to make sure you were okay. Then I overheard."

"And what I said makes you think you should help me. With what? I can take care of myself. Been doing that for a long time before I met you." He snorted. "It's me who's helping you."

"I know." I sat down in the chair next to him, letting my leg brush against his. He didn't move away, and that made me feel braver. I pushed my knee against his leg, sliding to the edge of my chair until I might as well have been in his lap.

"But you've never had to deal with a fire like this, have you? Everyone's talking about how this is the first time something this extreme has happened here. It's stressful for you, and I'm in the way. That's why I want to do what I can to help, to make up for taking up resources."

"You're talking like you're a parasite." Lance picked up one of the muffins and studied it, then put it back down on the plate and sighed. He pushed one of his big, strong hands back through his hair.

Dark strands stood up straight. I experienced an urge to smooth them down. "Martin, having you cook and clean is more than I could ask for. You don't need to do anything else. You're under stress, too."

"I want to do more," I insisted, and put my hand on his knee. I felt the way his thick muscles pushed against the material of his jeans, straining the seams. It was a wonder his clothes didn't fly off him every time he flexed.

Lance picked up my hand and put it on the table in front of me. A rejection. Like I'd rejected him before. "Earlier, when I kissed you, you pushed me away. Now you're trying to seduce me? Do you always have this much trouble making up your mind, or is this your normal tactic for getting someone to sleep with you?"

"I … I didn't say anything about sleeping with you," I sputtered. Even though that was exactly my plan, it threw me off to have him say it before I was ready. I'd been planning to work my way up to that.

Lance glanced over at my hand, which still lay limply on the table. "Seemed to me like you were going straight for the goal just now."

"I mean, I didn't say it *yet*. I was going to…"

"Why the change in heart?" he demanded. "No before, yes now."

"I can't explain it! I just want it!"

"Prove it," he challenged. His eyes were vibrant green under hooded lids, his pupils dilated. "Prove it to me beyond a shadow of a doubt. Then maybe I can trust you."

How could I prove it to him? I'd already said everything I could think of.

It was time to show him.

His hand was still wrapped around mine. I turned my hand, grabbing his fingers. I guided his hand to my lap, held it there while I pressed myself against him. Having this man touching me anywhere made my loins tighten instantly and my dick stirred to life. I arched my back, rubbing on his fingers.

"Feel that?" I whispered. "Does that prove it for you?"

Lance's eyelids lowered. His nostrils flared, like a wild animal scenting prey. He pushed the heel of his hand into my crotch, grinding against me.

I bucked my hips, letting out a gasp of delight as flashes of pleasure pulsed behind my eyes. The sensation translated into color, vivid shades I had never seen before and would never see again outside of this moment. A whimper rose up into my throat. I grabbed the table, bracing myself.

"Feels like you need something," Lance growled. The low thrum of his voice reverberated in my chest. I felt like I couldn't breathe.

"I need you," I gasped.

Lance wrapped his arm around my back and pulled me into his lap. I gasped again, feeling his desire pushing up against my ass. I wriggled around, grinding myself on him.

He moaned and slid his hand up into my hair. His lips crashed down hard on mine. My hands fluttered, settled against his chest.

I gripped his shirt, held onto him tightly while straining against him. I pressed my mouth more firmly against his, seeking out his tongue. Our tongues met, pushing together, playing, imitating an intimate act. A harbinger to what was coming, I hoped.

"You drive a hard bargain," Lance whispered against my lips. He kissed me again and I melted against him, my heart pounding in my chest. "But I think I need some more convincing."

He was teasing me. This strong, wild man was teasing me. I squirmed in his lap, pushing against his erection. He groaned and tossed his head back, and I took advantage, bringing my lips to his neck and kissing the hollow of his throat.

I let him feel my teeth nibbling his sensitive skin. He tasted of musk and salt, like hard work. His stubble was rough on my cheeks and lips, adding another level of sensation to the dozens of feelings already coursing through my body.

I nipped at him again, moving my mouth to his shoulder, right next to his neck, where a large stretch of muscle flexed. Something instinctive rose up inside me and I nipped him there, harder, adding pressure. Biting him, making him writhe underneath me, crying out with a mixture of pleasure and pain.

His hand in my hair tightened, tugging on my head. His other hand grabbed at my ass, squeezing my cheek, sending more waves of pleasure through me.

Suddenly, he stood up. His hand underneath my ass held me up, supporting me. One of his fingers pressed between my cheeks and I wrapped my legs around his waist, trying to relieve the pressure before I went crazy from need.

"We're going to break the chair if we just sit here," Lance growled. "Time to move."

He headed for the living room. I clung to him, trembling, feeling my dick push against his hard abs with every step.

He sat down with me on his lap, his hands roaming over my body while kissing me. I struggled to keep up with all of the sensations flooding my body, chasing his lips with mine. Everywhere he touched, I felt like he was spreading fire through me.

I pressed against him, sliding my hands down his arms, his muscular sides. I grabbed at the hem of his shirt, toyed with it, and slid my hands up underneath, stroking over the hills and valleys of his muscles.

He was built like a god, and even the act of touching him made me even more excited. My dick hurt, that's how hard it was pushing against my jeans.

Lance's lips jumped from my mouth to my ear. He caught my earlobe, sucked on it, tugged. "I think I believe you," he growled.

I couldn't find the words to say anything back. Instead, I found his nipple underneath his shirt and brushed my thumb over it. The turgid peak was hard and erect, and also velvet-soft.

Lance arched his back, and then I suddenly found myself on my back with him crouched over me, his hand working hard against my crotch. Shaking, I whimpered and cried out at the hot, intense feelings of pleasure. A primal need rose inside me and I grabbed suddenly at his wrists, clutching him, struggling to keep control of myself.

"I can't," I gasped. "I can't hold on much longer."

Lance kissed me so roughly I felt my heart starting to skip beats. "You have to hold on," he growled. "For a lot longer. I'm nowhere near done with you yet. If you're going to give yourself to me, I'm going to take all I can get. Wait here."

His last sentence came out of nowhere compared with everything else he was saying. I hadn't figured out what he meant when he stood up and hurried out of the living room. He walked like there was something impeding him and I smiled, knowing what it was.

It felt amazing to know I could have this kind of power over someone. The rest of my life was nothing like this.

While Lance was off doing whatever he was doing, I decided to take matters into my own hands. Standing up, I undressed as quickly as I could. My swollen dick slowed me down, and I had to move myself out of the way; even the slightest touch was almost enough to send me blasting off into orbit.

I could see the reflection of the outline of my body in the blank television screen. Compared to Lance, I was shapeless and boyish. There wasn't much of me to offer. Could he really be having such intense feelings for me?

In the end, it didn't matter. I was making him feel good, and that was what I cared about.

And I was feeling good, too.

Lance came back in another few moments, carrying lube in one hand. He stopped in his tracks when he saw me, his mouth opening with surprise. "You…"

Shaking his head, he tossed the lube onto the couch and tore off his shirt, revealing his muscles in all their glory. Seeing his body under his shirt, and feeling his muscles with my hands, couldn't compare with seeing him directly. He was gorgeous, in a way for which there weren't any proper words.

A thick thatch of curly black hairs covered his chest, just out of my reach before. A trail of hairs also led down from his navel to under the waistband of his jeans.

What was out of sight was quickly revealed as he removed the rest of his clothes. His cock sprang to attention, a marvelous length of tumescence. His cherry-red tip oozed with droplets of precum.

I dropped to my knees in front of him and brought my mouth to him. I slid my tongue over the head of his cock, tasting his essence. Wrapping my lips around him, I started to suck on him for more. My body needed it, cried out for it.

This, I had done before. I knew how to do it, and I would give it everything I had, just for him.

Lance stopped me with an impatient tug on my hair. I looked up at him, a little confused. My answer came in the form of being forcefully lifted up by my shoulders and tossed back onto the couch.

I bounced on the supple cushions, and then Lance was over me again, our naked flesh slapping together as he pounced. The tip of his cock burned against my ass opening, sending more fire through my entire body. Moaning and gasping, I grabbed at his hips and tried to impale myself on him.

Lance placed his hand on my chest, stopping me. "You're tight," he growled.

I blinked rapidly, trying to remember how words work. "I am?" was all I could come up with.

"You ever done this before?"

I blushed a little, which was probably enough of an answer. "I've sucked cock and fooled around. But I haven't … not with anyone."

The guys I picked up at the bar were usually fooling-around guys, which was fine with me. I didn't trust a stranger enough to let them near my ass. The few relationships I'd had usually fizzled out before they got intense enough for me to want to go all the way.

My partners always moved on, stating that we were in different places. I lacked the confidence to keep up with them, was what that meant.

Lance was staring down at me like I'd performed a magic trick, his sexy, hazy eyes wide with wonder. "You're a virgin?"

"Kind of?" Oral sex was still sex, but I had my anal virginity, if he wanted to think of it in those terms. "Is that okay?"

"And you still want to … you don't want to wait for someone special?"

I laughed. Wrapping my hands around Lance's face, I brought him down to me for a kiss. I didn't answer out loud; instead, I tried to let my convictions carry over to him in this format.

It must have worked, because I felt fingers pushing against my opening, asking for permission to enter. Bracing myself by holding onto Lance, I pushed back at him and felt his probing finger slide just inside me. The sensation was glorious, and I whimpered, bucking at him to try to get him in deeper.

He withdrew his finger and then pressed in again a moment later. Entrance was easier this time, accompanied by a slick, cold sensation. Lube.

Arching my back, lifting up my ass, I moved against Lance while he moved within me. His finger quested inside me like a voyager in a strange land, rubbing every part of me within reach, investigating me.

The unfamiliar feeling of being touched from within soon started to feel natural, even if it was still a little uncomfortable. My dick throbbed the entire time, and I kept having to fight against the urge to tense up. Whenever I did, Lance froze his finger in place inside me, and then bent over me to kiss me. I soon loosened up again, and the process of chasing ecstasy resumed.

An orgasm was building inside me, a fraction of pressure at a time. I could feel heat climbing up the shaft of my dick, threatening to burst out of me in a supernova.

"Lance," I gasped.

Either he felt me starting to shake out of control, or else he sensed the urgency in my voice. He slid his finger out of me and replaced his touch with the slick, lube-covered tip of his cock. He burned me, even through the layer of lube, which also warmed rapidly.

Having him pressed up against me like this was so good that my eyes closed and I saw stars in the darkness. Bursting stars, like fireworks. My control was slipping.

My breath came faster. I grabbed at Lance, dug my fingers into his back.

He entered me, sliding inside.

Progress was smooth for a few inches. The feel of him gliding inside me, rubbing on me from within, made me cry out and writhe in pleasure. Then he stopped.

"Loosen up," he gasped. "Relax for me. Let me in. More."

I tried as hard as I could to relax. Lance pushed in another few inches, stopped again. He started to pull out at that point, and a cry of disappointment tore from my throat. I clawed at his back, trying to forcefully bring him back inside me.

He pushed back inside, moving past the previous stopping point. He moved back again, and then forward once more, and by that time I understood what was happening. I started to move with him, struggling to match his slower speed, when all I really wanted to do was race ahead as fast as possible.

Lance kept pressing his way deeper inside me, his body rocking above me. I looked up at him while moving with him, and I realized with a start that I adored the way he looked. His lips were parted, grunting gasps of air bursting from his mouth. His eyes were half-closed with desire and concentration. He looked focused and intent, like he was on a mission and enjoying every step of the way.

He moved deeper inside me one last time, and I felt his hips push flush against my ass. We were fully joined, as close as two men could ever be.

The tip of his cock was brushing against a place very deep inside me, so deep I hadn't even known it was there. It was a place that felt hot and white and bright, like a sun inside me. Wrapping my legs tighter around Lance, I started to thrust at him.

He met my pace and moved with me, and we started to pick up speed. Our bodies pushed together, away, together again. The only sound that could be heard was our gasping breath and the sound of our skin slapping together.

With each thrust, Lance struck that sun inside me. I felt my mind start to splinter, the heat rising to unbearable levels inside me. Then, with a final thrust, it was all I could take.

My orgasm exploded into existence, and I barely had time to hear myself cry out before a tide of pleasure rushed through me like an undertow, sweeping my awareness away with it. My eyes were clamped shut, and behind my eyelids I saw a galaxy of shifting stars, colors that could only be found in the space of the mind.

How long it took me to come back down from my trip to the cosmos, I didn't know. Awareness slowly flooded back in. I felt the couch underneath me, a soreness in my ass. Lance's body pressed heavily on mine, his weight not entirely uncomfortable. His breath puffed against my neck.

I felt something vibrating, almost like purrs. After a moment of confusion, I realized he was laughing.

"Something funny?" I whispered.

Lance's face came into view. He was smiling. It was the most genuine smile I had ever seen from him, crinkling up the corners of his eyes. "You know," he said, almost casually, "I think you're right about this. I feel really relaxed right now."

I laughed and wrapped my arms around him, hugging him. After a moment, he touched my hair and stroked me. I hadn't really figured out what I would want to do in the aftermath of having sex with him, but this seemed pretty okay to me.

Eventually, Lance did have to get up. I could feel his stomach rumbling against me, like an earthquake. As the last remnants of my orgasm faded, more normal emotions settled in.

When he returned to the kitchen, I followed, eager for him to finally try the muffins I'd made. I watched, breathless, as he brought a muffin to his mouth and bit down. Raw batter flowed out of the muffin, plopping onto the table.

I stared at the puddle of batter, dismay rising inside me. "I tried so hard."

Lance tossed his head back and laughed. "I appreciate the effort. Think I'll make some eggs instead, though."

I stuck the muffins back in the oven. Unfortunately, I was soon to learn that baked foods were not meant to take two separate trips into the oven. The muffins technically finished cooking, but they also dried out to the point where no amount of butter could save them.

Lance took one to the station the next day to treat the dogs. They liked it just fine, so he decided to keep the rest around. A bit of sugar and fat wasn't going to hurt such active animals.

In the end, even though things hadn't gone the way I planned, I didn't regret a single thing. In fact, I was looking forward to doing it all again.

Whenever Lance wanted me, I would be right here for him.

Chapter 9 - Martin

The new tactic the fire department tried turned into a disaster. Lance told me all about it. With the help of departments from the surrounding counties, they'd tried to form their own fire lines.

Creating their own controlled fires gave them a way to impede the progress of the existing fire. It couldn't burn what was already burned, so the theory was that it would run out of fuel and lose some of its strength.

Unfortunately, the fire was so large and so powerful that it just absorbed the fire lines and kept right on going. Two more neighborhoods had been forcefully evacuated, and a lot of other people had moved out of their own volition. Some businesses had closed their doors, due to their own proximity to the blaze. A lot of families were suffering.

Not everything was terrible, though. The story of the fire had reached regional news lines, and support was starting to trickle in.

I was just glad that we were getting any help at all. I didn't need any of it myself, but it was heartening to hear about affected families being given donations and important supplies. Red Bluff's mayor started up some food drives, which helped to feed people.

Though we were knocked down, we kept crawling along.

I went to work for my next shift in high spirits, thinking idle thoughts about Lance and the way he made me feel. I replayed images of our sex in my mind, imagining his fingers sliding on my skin, running through my hair. I pictured the determined pre-orgasm look on his face.

All that not-paying-attention came back to bite me when I turned down the road in the business district where Pet Central was located. Something seemed a bit off, and I paused, letting my foot slip off the gas while trying to figure it out. It seemed like there was quite a lot of activity going on around the pet store. I racked my brain, trying to remember if there was some sort of sale I'd forgotten about.

And then I smelled it. It came in through the air conditioning vents in my car, thick and pungent.

Smoke.

Alarm lodged in my throat like I'd swallowed something too large. I jammed my foot back down on the gas pedal and drove as fast as I could to reach the parking lot. The closer I got, the more there was for me to see.

The bustling activity wasn't a result of customers at all. The parking lot was almost entirely empty, except for some employee vehicles, a few of which I recognized. Quincy's jeep. My manager's blue motorcycle. Haley's second-hand Mustang. Regular stuff.

But that was about where the expected stuff ended, and the mystery began. A police car was parked next to either entrance to the parking lot, both of which had been blocked off with orange traffic cones. Traffic was being redirected around the blockages, which was what was causing most of the disturbances.

In front of the store itself were three white vans, the kind you always heard about in abduction cases. I half expected to see creepy men wandering around, offering employees candy if they'd come inside the van. Instead, what I saw was my manager and my co-workers huddled around the front of the store, along with some blue-uniformed men who must have been the van's drivers.

What the hell was going on?

I pulled up beside the blocked-off entrance and rolled my window down. As expected, a cop got out of the cruiser and came up to me. "Move on, son," he said.

His voice was kindly. He *looked* kindly. With a potbelly and graying hair and a thick handlebar mustache, he looked like a gunslinger who had settled down and gone into retirement. "You're blocking traffic. Store's closed, anyway."

"I work at Pet Central," I said. I pointed to my vest, which lay on the passenger seat. "I have to get in there and see what's going on. Can you let me through, please?"

Always say please. Manners went a long way. I'd learned that being polite could solve a lot of problems, so at least my parents couldn't say they'd never taught me anything.

The old cop looked indecisive. He leaned in closer, lowered his voice. "I'll let you through. Only because you've been polite."

I kind of didn't expect this to work. He must have been extremely tired, or something. I didn't care enough to ponder on it very much.

The cop continued, "But, if I was you, I'd go home and call in sick today. It doesn't look good over there."

With the stench of smoke even stronger in the air now that my window was rolled down, I could guess what was going on. I also knew I couldn't go anywhere while it was happening. I'd cared for those animals. I needed to be there.

"Please let me through," I said. Still polite, though it was no longer a question.

The cop sighed and nodded, then moved away to pick up the cones so I could drive into the parking lot. In the few brief seconds it took him to do that, I took a closer look at the sky.

Anyone who had ever been in a car at all in their life knew that the windows darkened things. Their thickness turned light hazy, dulled colors. That was why I hadn't noticed what was above me until it was almost too late.

A thick film of hazy gray smoke blanketed the business district. The wind was strong, shoving the smoke around into intricate spirals and curls. The influence of the fire had finally reached here.

The animals were in danger.

I lifted my hand to the cop in thanks as I drove through the gap he'd made for me. I parked next to my manager's motorcycle, leapt out of the car, and ran over to the entrance. The group from before was dispersing and everyone was moving with purpose, hardly sparing me a glance.

My manager, Chris, saw me. He was normally the picture of a put-together young man, with slicked-back hair and immaculate dress. Today, he looked rumpled and frumpy, and his name tag was on backwards. Appearances were secondary to the health of animals.

Chris motioned me over to him. "We're evacuating the stock. All stock. Even the ones in the back."

The ones in the back were usually injured and needed recuperation time, or they were old animals we couldn't sell, or ones who were from an accidental litter who were too young. We might also have animals back there who needed some time to calm down before being put out on the sale floor. We usually didn't move those animals before they were ready, but this was a matter of life and death.

"Use the emergency crates from the back. If we run out of those, get crates from the vans. We're going to be moving everything to shelters, other stores, temporary foster homes. I've got that all arranged.

"Right now, we just need them out of there. You go to the adoption section."

"Right," I said, and hurried off. The adoption section would be a piece of cake. All the animals we had in there had originally been transported to us in crates and carriers. I could just use those.

The scene inside Pet Central reminded me something of a natural disaster movie, where people always raid store shelves, grabbing everything and anything they can. The difference was that there were a lot less people in here, and they were nabbing animals and bags of pet food instead of supplies meant for humans.

Quincy had his hand stuck in the mouse tank, chasing around tiny rodents, who were experts at not being caught. Haley hustled by with her arms dangerously full of betta fish containers. The colorful bettas swam in circles while she walked, looking around at their environment.

I took an immediate right once I was inside, following the wall to the other side of the building and from there to the adoption center, where animals from local shelters had a chance at finding a new place to live. Grabbing hold of the Employee Access door, I yanked it open, stepping into the back hallways.

A closet full of food and toys to the left. The animals to the right, who were rousing and stirring from all the commotion. A parrot squawked, an infamous macaw named Houdini because he had a habit of escaping from his new homes until the owners gave up on him.

Disturbed by the ear-splitting squawk, the kittens started mewling their fear and distress. I heard tiny hisses. A moment later, the full-grown cats followed suit.

Like a chain reaction, excited by the mewling of cats, who were fun to chase, the dogs started barking.

Dogs.

I froze in place in the doorway, staring in at the cages. I had forgotten about the dogs.

There were three of them. Two dachshund mixes and a little yapping terrier, the only one of his litter to survive when they were dumped on the side of the road in the heat. While the other animals huddled up in a corner, or moved around searching for a means of escape, the dogs stood at the front of the cages with all their attention focused on me.

Unease climbed up my spine. I felt like I couldn't breathe. An impending sense of failure started snapping at my heels, chasing me exactly as a herding dog might.

All I had to do was get the dogs into crates. If I opened the doors of the cages and held the crates up in front of the opening, they would go right in. I didn't have to touch them. I hardly had to look at them.

But they were looking at me. My stomach twisted inside me, painfully, and I grimaced.

The racket continued on, and now Houdini was whistling the tune to Spongebob Squarepants, rattling his beak on the bars in time with the music. My ears hurt; my lungs ached.

I pulled in a deep breath and tried to take a step closer to the animals. I could start with the others and end with the dogs, giving them my full attention. I could do it. I'd been spending so much time in the presence of Lance and his two huge Dalmatians, so I could definitely deal with two wiener mutts and a little puppy.

I could.

But, try as I might, I couldn't get my foot to lift up off the ground. I was stuck in place, glued there by a fear so ingrained in me that I was utterly powerless.

"I thought this would happen."

I turned to see Chris standing behind me, his arms folded. I hadn't even heard him walk up. "Chris..."

He sighed. "I want to say I'm disappointed, but I'm really not. As soon as I remembered that we had dogs back here, I knew you wouldn't be able to do it. I'll take over here. Go help evacuate the birds. They're most at risk."

Shame blossomed inside me like a spreading patch of blood, like I'd been stabbed. Lowering my head, I brushed past Chris and went to the birds. Someone else was already there, using a net to nab parakeets and stick them in little plastic carriers.

I fell in with them without a word, doing the same for the finches and wrens. All of our birds were purchased from breeders who hand-fed them as babies, meaning they were nearly tame already. However, tameness faltered in the face of panic, and the poor birds weren't making this easy on themselves.

I should have been more focused on the task at hand. It was a miracle none of the birds flew away from me.

In a time of emergency, I had proven myself to be completely worthless.

My career stopped here.

Chapter 10 - Lance

I paced in the kitchen, ignoring Martin as he walked up to watch me. Pushing my hands into my hair, I scowled down at the tiled floor.

"You okay?" Martin asked.

I turned to look at him and frowned. "No. I'm not okay. And I don't want to talk about it."

"But I could…"

"It's about the dogs. You can't do anything, so leave me alone."

His shoulders slumped, and he left to go sit on the couch. I watched as he picked up one of his games and started to poke at the screen before I resumed pacing around. He seemed to be in a lower mood than usual.

I wasn't the only person with problems. I was being selfish. Heading over to him, I sat down at his side and placed my hand on his knee.

"I'm sorry. That was rude of me. I'm kind of on edge, but it wasn't okay to take it out on you."

Martin glanced up at me and smiled. He leaned his head on my shoulder for a moment, his hair soft on my neck. "I forgive you. You don't have to talk if you don't want to. Just know I'm here for you if you do."

"You're so accepting," I murmured. "It's sweet." Even sweeter was watching his face light up with a blush.

What really bothered me was the lack of news from that lawyer, which told me that things weren't looking so good. My patience was running out. I was one man, trying to find a loophole to take advantage of a government-run facility.

It didn't matter that that government was local, or that I was a hard-working member of that facility. There were laws and regulations in place for this exact reason.

My options were to keep paying this stupid lawyer to be unhelpful, or try taking matters into my own hands.

The decision had haunted me for hours, and I suddenly couldn't stand to sit still any longer. Striding across the living room, I grabbed my truck keys.

Martin looked over at me, his brown eyes curious. "What are you doing?"

"I'm going to the station."

Martin blinked, and some clarity came into his eyes. He sat up, frowning. "Why? It's still the middle of your day off, isn't it? Did something happen?"

"I just realized I have some business I need to take care of," I grunted. I could have confided in him, but this was my fight, and mine alone. No need to get him mixed up in this.

"Do you want me to come with you?" Martin started to stand up.

I held out my hand, stopping him. "No. It has nothing to do with you."

He sat back with a frown on his lips. "Okay, but you know where to find me."

I smiled for him. "Yeah, I do."

I headed over to the front door and stuck my feet in my shoes, not bothering to properly untie and tie the laces. I wasn't going out to work, where perfection was one of the few defenses against certain death.

"Aren't you going to take the dogs?" Something in Martin's voice sounded hollow. I looked over at him, narrowing my eyes. Something must have happened today that had to do with dogs, or else there wouldn't have been such emphasis on that word. I felt awful for him, having that fear he couldn't control.

"No, I don't need to bring the dogs." I could at least help put some of his fears to rest. "They're in the bedroom, and they can't open doors. Plus, they're fast asleep. You won't have to interact with them at all."

"I'm sorry," Martin whispered. His cheeks burned red.

My heart twisted in my chest. I went back over to him where he sat on the couch. Holding his chin gently in my hand, I kissed his forehead, the tip of his nose, and his lips. I kept my lips against his and looked into his eyes. "Don't worry about it, okay?"

He nodded and lifted his hand. I caught it and squeezed it, then turned to go again. He didn't stop me this time, and I hoped that meant he felt a little better.

Once I got to the station, I headed straight for the chief's office. He was practically living in there these days. I knocked a little harder than I meant to, nerves getting to me.

I growled under my throat and tried to remind myself that I had to be in control if I wanted this to work. Brute force and aggression wouldn't get me anywhere with this guy. I'd have to be clever.

It was going to be tough.

After a moment, Chief Patrick responded. "Come in." He sounded exhausted. Meanwhile, I'd had a nap and a few good meals on my day off. I could get the upper hand, here.

I stepped inside the office, shutting the door behind me to give us privacy.

The office was small, but its tidiness made it seem larger than it was. It looked like the sort of place that might have belonged to a college professor. Tall bookshelves with important-looking tomes lined the walls. A massive desk crouched in the middle of the floor, like a primeval beast whose back was studded with misshapen spines. Those spines were everything from a desk lamp, to a pencil caddy, to an impressive stack of papers easily two feet tall.

On the other side of the desk was Chief Patrick. He was bent over an open binder, scribbling busily inside it. His eyes flicked up to take me in, then back down to his work. "What are you here for, Lance?"

That wasn't what he would have said to any other firefighter. I was different. I was an arsonist.

I sat down in the chair opposite him. He paused and then sighed, setting his pen aside. "Okay. You have my full attention. What?"

"You can stop it with the tough guy act, Chief. I'm not here about that."

Surprise crossed Patrick's face, though he was quick to cover it up again. He was not a man given to expressiveness, with a broad and impassive face, so any lapses were easy to catch. He wore his heart on his sleeve — during the moments when he had a heart.

"Then what do you need?"

"I wanted to talk to you about Spot and Dottie."

"Our fire dogs. Yes, of course." Patrick placed his broad hands on top of his binder, folding them and leaning over them. "What about them? Is something wrong?"

"They're both tired, but strong. They're always ready for work."

"That's good. You're a good caretaker, Lance."

"That's what I came here to talk about." Unease rose inside me, and I fought it down again. I couldn't show any weakness here. "I want to be more than just their caretaker."

Patrick said nothing.

"Look, Spot and Dottie are invaluable. They're clever and strong. They need a steady environment. All this going back and forth from one location to the other is harmful to them. If they stayed with me full-time, they'd have the stability they need."

"What are you saying?"

Here was where I probably should have prepared some sort of eloquent, heart-wrenching statement that would win him over to my cause without a doubt. Unfortunately, I'd done no such thing, and hadn't even thought about preparing what to say up until right now.

Guess I'll just have to get it all out there.

"I want to be their owner. Their real owner. Sign them over to me. Give me custody."

Patrick blinked slowly. It was a reptilian blink, the movement of a cold-blooded predator calculating his next move. "How long has this desire been growing inside you?"

It was my turn to say nothing. I wasn't going to reveal that I had wanted these dogs for myself ever since I picked them out.

They hadn't even had their eyes open at the time. Their weight was nothing in my hands. Yet they felt warm and alive, and I could sense their potential. I'd fallen in love with them.

"If you had brought this up sooner, it might have gone easier. You wouldn't have had all this time to build up your expectations, only to be disappointed by reality." Patrick leaned back in his chair, moving his hands so they rested on his stomach now.

He had a not-inconsiderable gut, which he'd been cultivating for the past several years. The tragic deaths of his wife and daughter in the not-so-distant past had taken quite the toll on him. Some would have even gone so far as to say he was unfit to be chief in the aftermath of that grief.

"So, that's a no. You aren't going to listen." Anger rose inside me. I struggled to keep ahold of myself. "I want what's best for these dogs."

"And I want what's best for my fire department. These dogs are much more than just workers. They're mascots, the face of the department. Everyone forgets what a fireman looks like when he's not in a sexy calendar, but they never forget about the dogs. They bring attention and support to us."

"They can't do that if they die from stress," I argued. I clenched my fists under the desk, where he wouldn't see them and feel threatened into action. My nails bit into my palms.

"These two are dogs in the prime of their lives. You're exaggerating, and that isn't helping your case."

Patrick gestured at his window, which offered a view of the street. A few cars passed by, their headlights cutting across the darkness. "Opinions matter. When you signed up for this job, you knew the reason you were getting into it.

"The public's perception of this department can make or break us. You've worked hard to increase that support. The dogs do the same. You'd best let this go, or someone might suddenly discover there's more to you than meets the eye."

I swallowed hard. My palms were sweaty, clammy from tension.

"If something were to happen to you, I would have to hand Spot and Dottie over to someone else. You would hate for that to happen, wouldn't you?"

The dogs were trained to respond to commands from anyone, hence why even babies could get them to do tricks. I wasn't technically needed any longer. If I pushed my luck, Patrick would push back, and then that would be it for me.

"Of course, if I gave the dogs to someone else, there's the possibility of them acting out. They might bite someone, endanger someone. I'd be forced to have them put down."

I lurched to my feet, slamming my hands down on the desk. Papers fluttered to the floor. I tasted salt on my lip where I was biting it, drawing blood. "How fucking dare you?"

Patrick looked at me with an eerie, extreme calm. He wasn't bluffing. I felt cold, so cold, as if I'd fallen through the ice over a frozen lake.

"As much as I would hate to do that, it could become necessary. If you don't want that to happen, it seems like you had best leave this be."

I turned my head away. My heart pounded. I felt my nostrils flaring, like a wild animal scenting for danger, but all I could smell was my own fear.

It took everything I had in me to be able to force out a single word. "Fine."

"Fine what?'

"I understand what you're saying."

"Good. Now, if there's nothing else, could you please leave? I have some things I should have read and signed yesterday, and I would like to catch up on them."

I stood up and walked over to the office door, being sure to step on his important papers on the way out.

"Lance?"

What now?

Patrick smiled when I looked back at him, a cat who'd gotten into the cream. "Any concerns you have, you can always bring them to me."

Rubbing his victory in my face.

I got out of there before I said anything that would piss him off and get me arrested. I hadn't lost my temper, but I hadn't succeeded. In fact, I had upped the stakes and made everything worse.

I felt drained as I drove back home. Anger brewed in my stomach like a storm cloud, humid and fierce.

I wasn't going to give up. I just needed to get smarter, somehow.

Chapter 11 - Martin

After the muffin fiasco, I was taking no chances. Instead of baking a cake, I bought one from the bakery. The expense bothered me, especially since Pet Central was closed down, leaving me momentarily without a job, but I figured it'd be more expensive to keep baking cakes until I got a perfect one.

Lance had told me that there had been some success with the fire. The tides might finally be turning. Funds were pooled, resources gathered, and arrangements were made. It all culminated in the renting of a fire helicopter and a pilot to fly it.

I hadn't known fire helicopters were a thing, but apparently they were really common here in California. The chopper carried massive amounts of water up above the fire, and then let it all pour down.

The result was something like a flood. The force was not comparable to a fire hose, but the sheer quantity of water and the surface area affected made up for the lack of pressure.

The operation was carried out in the early hours of the morning, to keep rubbernecking and media presence at a minimum.

"When all that water came pouring down, the sun shone on it," Lance had told me. "It looked like the dawn was pouring out of the sky. Pink and orange and yellow."

The image conjured up was vivid, though I had no doubt that what I imagined was nowhere near as impressive as the real thing.

After several passes, which took place over a few long, hard hours, the fire had taken a huge hit. Since then, normal firefighting tactics seemed to be more effective, as the blaze had been robbed of some of its strength and fearsome heat.

That alone was reason to celebrate. I had been already on my way to the store to pick up something for dessert. There were posters and signs in the window, as always. Most of them announced daily specials and deals, or relayed local news and upcoming events.

In the middle of all the usual clutter was a massive hand-drawn poster, which turned out to be the result of the collaborative effort of all the kids who attended youth group at one of the local churches. The poster depicted a firefighter holding a hose, positioned in an unfortunate way so that it looked as if he was clutching his cock. The hose sprayed water on a group of square houses, which had red and yellow scribbled on them to represent flames.

There was text underneath the massive picture, written in a more adult hand. I read the words. "Thank a fireman today for keeping us safe. And wish a happy birthday to the firemen with birthdays this month."

That was followed by a list of three names. One of those names was Lance Williams. His birthday was listed as being in just a couple days.

This kind gesture from a group of kids had given me this brilliant idea, and now I had to act on it. I could kill two birds with one stone — only metaphorically, of course — by buying a cake to celebrate the victory over the fire *and* Lance's birthday.

Maybe I can get one more bird, too…

The cake was perfect. I thought Lance might not appreciate having something fire-themed shoved in his face. It was his job, not his entire existence.

So I had requested that the decorations on top of the cake should be of two Dalmatians, along with some words that read "Happy Birthday, Dad!"

It seemed like such a cute thing to do, to get the dogs in on it. Kind of, anyway.

Once I had the cake, I went over to Walmart and picked out some decorations. As it turned out, finding birthday decorations for grown men was difficult.

The selection was limited to children's party supplies, twenty-first-birthday-themed alcohol decorations, and ironic senior citizen adornments. There wasn't much that really catered to serious grown men who had their shit together and their entire lives ahead of them.

It also occurred to me that I didn't know how old Lance was going to be.

I picked out a small pack of number candles and dropped those into my cart, thinking *good enough.* I also bought a lighter, some birthday hats, which looked stupid but would be hilarious if I could get Lance to wear one, and some black-and-white spotted paper plates.

I picked up some balloons and a banner and also added those to my cart. If this ended up looking too stupid and childish, the cheap supplies wouldn't set me back too much.

Getting out of Walmart was much more difficult than getting in. I stood in line for one of three available registers, leaning on the handlebar of my cart and idly browsing the candy and snacks. *National Enquirer* was insisting that the president was an alien and the earth was flat, while a *Lifestyle* magazine promised to teach me how to effortlessly go vegan.

Finally, I got up to the register. The bored cashier muttered a greeting and started scanning my items. I fetched my card and stood there, occasionally shifting my feet. Walking around on hard tile wasn't fun. I felt bad for the cashiers who just had to stand there all day.

"Don't your feet hurt?" I asked.

The cashier glanced at me. She gave a little laugh while trying to find a barcode on the crumpled packaging of the birthday banner. "We've got little mats on the floor back here. They don't really help."

I knew what she was talking about. We had those at Pet Central. The mats were little more than those cheap rugs people put outside of their front doors for people to wipe their feet on. They didn't do shit.

I made a few more comments through the rest of the checkout process, trying to get another laugh out of the cashier. She smiled a few times, so it hadn't been a total failure.

I wished her a good day and headed out with my purchases, hoping that I had made her day a little easier. I always liked to make people feel good. On a day like today, when things were already looking up, I wanted to share a bit of my cheer with others.

I drove home faster than I should have, to ensure I got there before Lance. The success with the fire meant he was going to come home tonight, instead of early in the morning. I wanted to be ready for him.

Bringing my Walmart bags inside Lance's house, I headed for the dining room and got to work. The banner I'd chosen was striped with black and white, the closest they'd had to Dalmatian colors. It didn't look too stupid hanging on the wall, so I decided to leave it up.

I blew up the balloons, and that was more difficult than it should have been because I kept thinking about the last thing I'd blown. It hadn't been a real blow job, since we'd moved on to other activities, but my brain made the connection, and now I couldn't stop thinking about it. Hunger stirred inside me and I allowed myself to dwell on it, wondering if I would get another chance tonight to have Lance's big cock in my mouth.

I set up the rest of the directions and put the boxed cake in the middle of the table. When he came home, I'd call him in here and flip open the lid of the cake box so he could see what was inside.

I had other plans, too, but those were a little more abstract. I needed him here for those.

When I had done everything I could to prepare, I perched on the couch in the living room and waited. Excitement and anticipation made it hard to focus, and I didn't want to miss him coming home, so I didn't turn the TV on. I tried to read and kept getting distracted, my eyes moving back and forth over the same sentence without understanding what was written there.

The more time that passed, the more the anticipation built up inside me. I shifted around, restless. A high, tingling feeling settled in my throat, like a maddening itch I couldn't scratch.

My heartbeat thundered in my ears, making it difficult to hear. In fact, I missed the sound of Lance pulling up the driveway in the truck, and I didn't hear his truck door close, or his approach to the front door. All I heard was the sound of the lock being thrown.

All the excitement that had been gathering pressure inside me suddenly exploded, and I took off like a rocket, throwing myself into the dining room. I grabbed the lid of the cake box and threw it open.

I must not have been fast enough in my escape because Lance called out, "Martin?"

Having him witness my mad dash wasn't part of the plan, but there wasn't much I could do about it at this point. I called back, "Yes?" My voice squealed with excitement.

"You okay? Saw you run."

I could hear the dogs moving around, and I hardly cared, that's how eager I was for this to happen. "I'm okay. Can you come in here? I have something to show you."

"If it's more muffins, no thanks." He sounded like he was smiling, which made my heart warm. "Let me just get the dogs up and I'll be right there."

I waited, and soon he was approaching the kitchen, coming through the doorway, turning in the direction of the dining room. He paused, and I watched his turquoise eyes flit around the room, landing briefly on each decoration before finally coming to rest on the cake in the middle of the table.

"Happy birthday!" I said. I held up the pack of candles. "I know it's not the right day, but I wanted to celebrate early because of the success with the fire."

Lance stared at me, then a smile spread across his face. The color of his eyes lightened towards blue. His nose crinkled up, making me want to kiss the tip of it until he unscrunched it.

"I didn't expect this. I really didn't expect this. Martin … This is all very thoughtful. You didn't have to do this. The guys at the station usually get cupcakes to celebrate birthdays, and that's about it."

I blushed. "All I did was buy some cheap decorations."

"But you did it because you wanted to. Not because you thought you had to. That's the difference." Lance crossed the room and wrapped me in his arms, squeezing me.

I clutched him and lay my cheek on his chest, relishing the embrace and the feel of his body around mine. He was so solid, so strong. My dick stirred, awakened by interest.

"I would have put the candles on, but I don't know how old you are."

He chuckled and pulled back. "I'm going to be 27. God, I'm an old man, aren't I?"

"Pretty spry for an old guy," I commented. I ripped open the pack of candles and took out the two and the seven, sticking them into the cake. Lance had already grabbed the lighter. I reached out and took it from him. "You can't light your own candles."

"Why?"

Does he look a little pale right now?

I lit the candles. They were cheap ones, so it was no easy task. "My grandma always said that a wish won't come true if you light your own candles. Someone else has to do it, because it's their intent for you to be happy that gives the wish power."

"Interesting."

He definitely looked a little pallid, which was weird, given the circumstances. Maybe that was just the lighting, or he was tired from his long day. I pushed my misguided concerns aside. "I'm not much of a singer, so we should skip that part."

"Thank god. I hate that part." Lance grinned. He looked so rakishly handsome that it was hard to pay attention to his lack of color. "Can I make my wish now?"

"You probably should, before wax gets all over the cake."

Lance bent over and puffed at the candles. They went out in an instant, and little drifts of smoke puffed up from the blackened wicks.

"What did you wish for?" I asked.

Lance looked at me with his eyebrows raised. "Didn't that grandma of yours tell you that you have to keep your wish a secret, or else it won't come true?"

That was what I'd hoped he would say. I took a deep breath, gathered up what little courage I had, and asked, "Do you want to know what I wish for?"

Now his eyebrows drew together. "That's not how birthday wishes work."

"It is tonight. Because you can make my wish come true." My heart raced in my chest and I balled my hands into my fists. "I wish you'd go on a date with me tonight. Dinner, wine, the whole nine yards. What do you say?"

There was incredible hope in my heart as I gave voice to those words. I didn't think I was much of anything. I was a failure of a son, a failure of an employee.

My life was at a standstill, and I couldn't even go home. There were tons of other people who were more deserving of asking such a thing of him.

Even knowing all that, even knowing I was a piece of trash in human form, I couldn't forget the way he had looked at me when he kissed me, or the expression on his face when we'd had sex. There were these miraculous moments between us when we were so connected, and the rest of the world didn't matter at all.

I had to listen to what those moments meant. I had to pay attention to the way he made me feel.

I wanted to be the one he went to when he needed to talk. I wanted to see if there could be more than that between us. Things had been pretty easy up until now between us, so that had to mean something, didn't it?

Lance looked at me and said, "No."

Chapter 12 - Lance

Martin left.

I hated him for leaving, and I wished so much that he would have stayed and kept trying to convince me to go on a date with him. That was what he had done when he was trying to get me to rely on him for stress relief. He had persevered, though that seemed to go against his nature.

It went against mine too, which was probably how he'd managed to convince me in the first place.

Sitting at the table in front of that cake, while the candles cooled and the wax hardened, I put my head in my hands and tried to think. I wasn't much of a thinker, though. All I could come up with was that maybe this date had meant more to him than sleeping with me.

That didn't make sense, though, did it? Sex was intimate as hell. A date was something you did with someone you hardly knew. We'd gone past that point already.

So why had he asked in the first place?

I groaned and pushed my fists against my temples, as if I could force my brain to work better. Maybe those two points were reversed for him? Although I didn't know how the hell that would work.

It didn't make sense with the fact that he had been a virgin, either. If he always went straight for sex, he should have had someone other than me inside him.

Then again, I guessed it was unlikely for him to have encountered this situation before. It wasn't often that a complete stranger invited you into their home. All of this could just be a result of gratitude, except that seemed unlikely, too.

Sure, he was grateful to me, I knew that. But when we had had sex, he had been doing a whole lot more than just going through the motions. He had been an active participant, loving every second of it, like I had.

He had done this, all of this, everything, because he wanted to.

He wanted to go on a date with me. To … what? Take things a step further? He wanted to date, be a couple?

I was a family guy. Growing up with a country life, everything was so much simpler. Even without wanting to inherit the farm or marry my neighbor, I still had thought I'd someday find a love like my parents had. Easy. Natural.

I *did* someday want to have an omega husband, and an American Dream house with 2.5 kids. Was that what Martin wanted? Were our end goals the same? Did it matter at this point?

Growing frustrated, I grabbed the knife sitting on the table and stabbed into the cake. I cut out a thick piece and set it on one of those ridiculous childish plates, and licked icing from the knife. Picking up my fork, I pierced the cake and brought a forkful to my mouth.

The taste was as to be expected, sugar-sweet and cloying, with notes of chocolate from the cake itself. But as I chewed, something seemed to change. The cake turned bitter, and the texture became paste-like. Swallowing was difficult.

After that one bite, I pushed the rest of the cake away and got up from the table. I went to my bedroom, where Spot and Dottie were snoozing. Their ears pricked up as I entered, and they looked over at me, their brown eyes wide and glowing.

Moving almost as a single unit, the Dalmatians rose to their paws and sat at my feet. I stepped over them, heading for the bed, aiming to lie down. I sat on the edge and then stayed there without moving, feeling something familiar and dreadful form inside me.

Despair.

It was the taste of despair in my mouth. It was despair wrapping dark tendrils around my brain, preventing me from seeing the logic in things.

Spot jumped up and lay down on my left, with his head on my thigh. Dottie took the right, leaning her flank on mine. Their presence soothed some of the darkness inside me. Sighing, I rubbed my eyes and tried to think over things again.

The sex we had had wasn't intimate. It was an intimate *act,* but its purpose had been utilitarian. Stress relief. And that had worked well, because we were both attracted to each other, and could agree upon that course of action in the end.

A date was far more personal in this context, wasn't it? I thought that Martin might think that. A date meant we liked each other for more than the physical. A date meant ... well, just *more.*

Martin wanted more.

And some part of me had reacted and shut him down.

I slid my hand into Dottie's fur, and she let out a soft chuff while resting her beautiful head on my shoulder.

He was a good guy, a real cutie anyone would have loved to snatch up. Those golden curls, his slender frame, and the startling depth and intensity of his warm brown eyes. Each of those aspects was something which could cause someone to fall in love with him.

I felt like I had let something go that was vital to my existence. Like I had lost something so good.

Maybe I should get drunk. I'd feel better, looser.

But I didn't move. I sat there on the bed, and I thought about Martin.

Chapter 13 - Martin

The embarrassment of that rejection from Lance was going to be something that haunted me for the rest of my life. I couldn't believe that I'd thought he would go for someone like me. And all those stupid decorations and that ugly cake just made me look desperate for him to accept me. God, what a fucking idiot.

Tears wet my cheeks while I drove, heading nowhere. I sniffled and lifted one hand from the steering wheel to wipe my eyes, but my vision grew blurry again as more tears rose. The street in front of me was a chaos of splotches of light and dark. I couldn't tell what was another car and what was a stoplight.

Wiping my eyes again, I looked around for somewhere to stop and get ahold of myself. There was a bar nearby, it looked like. I was not a bar kind of guy, unless I was with a group of other people —- or unless I was looking to pick up someone to fool around with.

My solitude tonight seemed fitting. I'd drink alone and work at accepting my fate as someone who would never quite be good enough at anything to have success.

My heart ached, squeezing fresh, hot tears from my eyes. I blinked hard and pulled into the parking lot, navigating through the tight aisles until I found a spot. At least, it was a spot now.

Stepping out of my car, I headed over to the bar. Normally, I got carded right at the door. Tonight, no one stopped me. It must have been the look on my face. No one wanted to mess with me.

I got a beer and took it over to a booth far away from anyone else. I sat and watched condensation trickle down the outside of the glass, reminding me of my tears from only a minute ago. Shame crept up my spine on spindly, spidery legs at how badly I had failed in my endeavors tonight.

Grabbing my beer, I drank deeply. The taste was a little too bitter for me, since I wasn't usually much of a drinker, but there was an aftertaste of citrus that helped mellow things out. It wasn't half bad, so I took another deep swallow.

Warmth ignited deep in my stomach, a spreading pool of it that invaded my veins with a light, buzzing fire. The rest of the world faded away in the face of the sensations coming from inside me. I hardly heard the chatter of the other patrons, the pulsing bass of the music filtering in through the speakers.

Fuck Lance, I thought. I didn't really mean it, but it felt good to vent some of my frustration. I said it out loud. "Fuck Lance."

"Who's Lance?"

I almost dropped my beer. Twisting around, I saw my co-worker, Quincy. He held a cocktail glass in one hand. The other, down at his side, was wrapped in bandages.

"Forget Lance," I said. "What happened to you?"

"When I was getting all those rodents out of the store, they decided to express their displeasure." Quincy shrugged. "Can't blame them. I'd bite the giant hand chasing me around my house, too."

I grimaced. Hamsters, especially, could be nippy, but it was usually a grab-and-let-go kind of thing. A scared or pissed-off hamster would chomp down as hard as it could, though. Same for mice and gerbils and even our placid guinea pigs. "That has to suck."

"Can't suck as much as whatever you're dealing with." Quincy sat down opposite from me, setting his cocktail in front of him. He had a tattoo on the back of his uninjured hand that I had never noticed before. A woman's name. Samantha. "Who's Lance and what do I have to do to him?"

I frowned. "Do to him?"

"Yeah. Like, tell me what he did to you so I can get back at him." Quincy flashed a grin. He was usually more of a solemn guy who only smiled when something was really funny, so I guessed that he might be drunk, or else was getting there.

"It doesn't matter," I sighed, and took another drink.

"Hey, fuck that. It does matter, you know? You're one of the nicest people I've ever met. You don't deserve to have anyone upset you."

I blushed a little and looked down. "I'm not that nice."

"Bullshit. You've never met a person you won't talk to. You make everyone feel special, and you remember shit that no one else ever would."

I did like companionship, and I did like having people to talk to. Hell, even now, in the depths of my despair, I was enjoying having Quincy to talk to instead of being by myself.

"But what's the point?" As quickly as my enjoyment had come, it was gone again. "I'm nice. So what? I'm not special or anything. No one would ever look at me and think hey, I need to get to know that guy better."

Quincy snorted. "What about all the people who randomly come up to you to talk to you all the time?"

"Okay, and then we have a conversation for a few minutes, and then it's all over and that's the end."

"Man, whoever this Lance fuck is, he sure did a number on you."

I sighed and drained the rest of my beer. I felt the warmth of the alcohol finally reach my brain, loosening my thoughts a little. "No. It's been like this pretty much for my whole life.

"I'm nothing special, and I keep trying to act like I am, and I get disappointed. Work, family … crushes. It all turns out the same. I fail. I don't listen. I fail again."

Quincy waved a waitress over and requested another round for the both of us. It was nice of him, though I should probably be careful not to actually get drunk. I'd already done something stupid tonight. I didn't need encouragement to do it again.

Once we both had our drinks, Quincy looked intensely into my eyes. "Look, you listened to me way back at the beginning of the year. Remember? When I was having problems with Sam."

I did remember, vaguely. The two of them had been dating for years, and things had suddenly started going south. Disagreements arose from nowhere and the two had been on the verge of a breakup.

"You told me we should take a break. Try to think about things differently. We spent some time apart, thought about some things, and now I'm going to propose to her on her birthday in a month. I already got this."

He lifted his hand to show off the tattoo, still raw and red around the edges. "Taking some time made me realize how important she was to me. Being in different places, having issues. All that didn't mean shit in the end. I love her, and that's all that matters."

"I'm glad for you," I said. Hearing his love success story made me hurt on the inside, a knife twisting in my gut. I'd never have something like that.

"Thanks, but I'm not talking about this just to talk about it. I'm trying to give you advice, like you gave it to me. Take a break, Martin."

Quincy looked at me. Though his eyes were fever-bright with the effect of at least two cocktails in his system, he looked solemn and serious as always. He meant what he was saying.

"Don't, like, quit, but take a break. Think about the obstacles, and how you can get around them. Accept what you can't change, because there has to be a reason it's like that. Right?

"Try to work on things with Lance. And if he hurts you again, tell me and I'll kick his ass."

Maybe I was a little more buzzed than I had thought, or maybe the idealistic nature of Quincy's speech resonated with that stupid, naïve part of me that kept trying even when it should quit. Either way, it got me thinking.

Was there a way to make this right, for both myself and Lance? Something existed between us. If a date wasn't the right way to start bringing us closer, then I'd have to think of another way to do it.

I couldn't do my thinking while I worked, which was when I had my best ideas. And I couldn't go back to Lance's house and do it there, because he'd be a distraction.

That left one place.

"You look like you're pretty deep in thought," Quincy said.

I looked up at him and smiled. "Yeah. You've really got me thinking. Throwing my own words back at me."

Quincy nodded and smiled back. "You do seem like the kind of guy who wouldn't follow his own advice. You're too fucking hard on yourself."

I was hard on myself because I had to be. That was what I'd been raised to know.

Maybe it was time for that to change?

Quincy and I talked for a little longer, though we didn't have much to say. He eventually excused himself and said that he'd best get home. He was trying to find work, and had an interview tomorrow morning in a city about half an hour away from Red Bluff.

I need to do that.

I resolved to do it tomorrow. Maybe I needed to take a break from working with animals, give myself some time to figure that out, instead of always pushing it.

I wished him luck and finished drinking my beer, taking my time to let some of the stirring and whirling of my thoughts settle down.

Standing up was easy enough, and I wasn't too unsteady on my feet, so I figured I'd be safe to drive.

I needed to go home. I needed to be away from Lance, and back in my element. With the recent successes in the fight against the fire, it'd be safe to go there for a little while, wouldn't it?

Hopping in my car, I drove in the direction of my neighborhood. Curls of smoke wreathed past the rising moon like clouds, but there was a lot less of it than there used to be. Encouraged, I kept driving.

In my mind, I was already sinking down in my own bed, luxuriating in the comfort of home. Yeah, this was going to be just what I needed.

Chapter 14 - Lance

Sitting around was going to drive me fucking insane. If I had to listen to myself go over the same point, the same thought, one more time, I might as well go to the hospital and have myself committed to a psych ward. There was only so much circling a stupid guy like myself could take.

Like a lot of stupid guys, I felt better when I was doing something physical.

I let Spot and Dottie out, and then left them at home, giving them free rein of the place for the first time since I'd invited Martin to come live with me. They probably wouldn't care, though. Sleep was the one thing on their minds right now.

I took the truck to the station and parked in the lot, which was a little fuller than it had been for quite some time. Now that we no longer needed every hand working around the clock against the fire, some of the newer members of the department had been reassigned to regular duties, which included answering calls and performing maintenance. Normalcy.

Even though I was currently on my off-hours, I figured the newbies wouldn't mind if they got some help. Get a bunch of men in one place for a prolonged period of time, and it was pretty easy to tell that we hadn't been properly taught how to clean up after ourselves. Our few female firefighters didn't pick up after us, as they shouldn't.

Some of the others thought differently, but me, I was still a farm boy deep inside. You could take me away from the corn-husking, the hoeing, the dawn-rising and the cow-milking, but you couldn't take those things out of my spirit.

Man, woman, didn't matter. You did your fair share, and expected everyone else to do the same, so you didn't have to pick up their slack.

I might've been about to break that rule by offering extra help, but it was more for me than them. A few hours of cleaning, followed by some exercising at the in-station gym, and I knew I'd feel better.

I headed inside, and the first thing I saw was Shepherd. He had a small janitorial cart at his side, one of the yellow kinds that came complete with an attached mop bucket. He was busily mopping, slopping soapy water in alarming quantities all over the floor.

"The hell are you doing?" I asked.

Shep looked up at me and smiled. "Lance! Hey! It's just like old times, huh?"

I folded my arms. "By old times, you mean a few weeks ago."

"Is that all? It feels like a whole lot longer than that." Shep shrugged. "Oh, well. Anyway, glad to see you're here. We haven't had a lot of time to talk recently."

"Right," I agreed. Although his enthusiasm seemed a bit overbearing, I couldn't deny that I was also happy to see him. He was the closest thing I had to a human friend, now that I'd ruined things with Martin.

With a start, I realized that I had missed having conversations with this annoying, bubbly man. It was difficult to think about anything bad when you were being pulled into his world. Sometimes I thought it must look like Candyland in his head, all bright colors and sweetness and clean fun.

Shep slopped water all over the floor, practically turning the entrance into a river. He seemed to have no idea how a mop worked, not that that was surprising. "Me, I've been mostly sleeping during my days off. You?"

"Sleeping and eating," I agreed. "Taking care of the dogs."

Shep dunked the mop back in the bucket and sloshed it all around. He pulled it back out, sopping wet, and didn't bother to wring out the excess before slapping the mop head back down on the floor. "Spot and Dottie! I've been seeing more of them than I have of you. They're all over the place. You really trained them well."

I had to grin. "Thanks."

Perfect topic. Couldn't think about Martin when I was thinking about my spotted loves.

"Hey, I heard something the other day," Shep commented. He lifted his bright eyes to mine, startling me. "I heard that you're thinking about trying to get the dogs for yourself. Why can't you just wait until they get retired? They're basically guaranteed to be yours, then."

I couldn't answer the question, because I was too busy reeling in surprise from the fact that he knew about that. I hadn't imagined the chief would tell anyone.

Then again, why not?

It had become abundantly clear in the past that he was not afraid of blackmail. Maybe, by spreading rumors, he was trying to stir up trouble.

"Lance?"

I snapped out of my shock with a twitch, hurrying to remember what was the last thing he had said. Spot and Dottie were around four years old. Working dogs tended to retire between seven and nine years of age, depending upon when they started to slow down and be less useful to their department.

If I waited for their retirement, I would have only a few years after that to enjoy owning them full-time. Maybe it was selfish, but I didn't want to wait. I didn't want *them* to have to wait. They deserved the best I could give them as soon as possible.

I didn't know how to say all that out loud to Shep, so I just said, "I don't know what could happen to them before then. And what if I wait all that time, and they end up not being mine at all?"

Shep frowned. "Sure, I guess that makes sense. Anyway, I wanted to tell you that I'll be a character reference for you."

A second surprise in as many minutes. Maybe I'd underestimated this guy. "What? Character reference?"

"Like…" Shep paused in his mopping, which was probably a good thing. He was even worse at it when he was talking.

"I think those dogs really should belong to you. It doesn't take a genius to see that. So, if you ever need someone to vouch for you that it'd be best if you own them, I'll do that for you."

This sudden display of generosity brought tears to my eyes. This never would have happened normally, but I was tired and vulnerable. I blinked rapidly and stared at Shep.

"What are you playing at?" I grunted. "Why would you do that?"

"Well, they trust you most." Shep shrugged, like that was so obvious he shouldn't even have to say it. "The way they look at you and come to you, it's obvious they love you.

"They look to you when they need a command. You're gentle with them. You know how they work. You're smart."

"That last one is a lie. And it doesn't have to do with anything, anyway."

I was not a smart guy. Never once in my life had I described myself in that way, and no one else had, either. I was the grumpy, gruff, aggressive guy who used intimidation to get my way.

Shep shook his head. "It takes someone smart to know what the dogs need before they even show it. You have all this stuff to remember about them, and you do it just fine. That's smart."

Doubt rose inside me, like air bubbles escaping from a sinking ship. I couldn't believe what he was saying.

"You know when people need stuff, too. You know when things should be done, and how. You can read a fire like no one else. Lance, you never noticed how everyone here looks to you for instructions?"

"I'm bossy."

"You're authoritative," Shep argued, using the biggest word I'd ever heard him say. "Sometimes, I think you should be chief. Anyway, I'll say all that if you ever need me to. Just let me know."

I still doubted what he said, although it was clear to me that he believed what he was saying. Smart. Authoritative. Words I never would have associated with myself.

Why not? asked a little voice inside me.

I knew what the dogs needed because I had worked with them so much. I knew how to read them.

And I knew how to read people. I could adapt to whatever they needed to get the job done, and I did.

Was that the same thing as being smart? I'd always thought of intelligence as being textbook. Topic-bound. Calculus was smart. Having knowledge about history was smart. Chemistry and biology was smart.

Knowing how to pay attention to people ... smart?

As for having authority, I just thought everyone obeyed what I said because they were intimidated by me. It had never crossed my mind they might respect me, or trust my decision-making skills.

If all of this was what Shep thought, others might think the same way.

Martin might have thought the same way.

I was more to him than just some guy who was doing him a favor, if that was true. And I had rejected him without giving him a chance.

I thought I'd been acting on my instincts, but maybe that wasn't the case. Maybe I'd done what I *thought* I should do, instead of what I *knew* I wanted to do.

In which case, I had really fucked up.

"Lance? You look constipated."

"That's my thinking face," I growled. I glared at Shep, who laughed.

"You should find a new thinking face, then. That one doesn't suit you."

"I'll keep that in mind."

I need to find Martin. I need to explain to him what's going on.

Urgency built inside me, and I turned away from Shep, about to push my way back out through the door and into the night.

"Where are you going?" Shep called.

I stopped and turned around. I smiled for him, trying to convey how grateful I was to him for this conversation. "You've made me realize something. I was going to stick around, but I have to go do something else while there's still time."

"Sure," Shep said, accepting what I said without question. I thought that willingness was probably just his nature, instead of being a response to whatever authority he thought I had. "We'll have to hang out some other time."

"Yeah. Maybe. But until we do, will you wring out that mop, for fuck's sake? You're going to flood the building."

"Wring out the mop?"

Exasperated, I headed over to him and snatched the mop handle from his hand. Lifting it up out of the water, I stuck it in the little basket area on top of the bucket and pushed the lever to squeeze out the excess water. Then I pushed it all back at Shep. "There."

Shep stared at the wringing basket and the lever as though he'd just discovered an alien. "*That's* what that's for! Oh, that's so much easier!"

Fucking hell, I thought, and left him to it. *He's a nice guy, but damn, he is clueless.*

I couldn't stick around to see what other cleaning-related deficiencies Shepherd might have. I'd already spent too much time talking to him, when what I really should have been doing was hunting after Martin.

I wanted a second chance. I was going to say yes this time, and we would talk and figure this out. I had discovered a part of me that was letting me see the situation with new eyes.

I had to see where this could go.

Chapter 15 - Lance

Hopping into my car, I started driving. Keeping half my mind on the road, I thought about how much of a connection I'd actually formed with Martin.

My attraction to him wasn't simply lust. I liked him for *him*, the way *he* felt. So small, so smooth, so soft against my body. He brought out the animal in me, made me feel like protecting him and claiming him all at once.

His brown eyes saw to the heart of me. I didn't like my heart, though. I shied away from looking too intensely at what he saw.

His tousled golden hair. To call him blond was the same thing as calling a dinosaur a lizard; while technically correct, the term didn't do justice to reality. The sun played on his locks as if it had found a long-lost friend.

The way he moved, the way he spoke, his attempts at conversation, his jokes, his continued interest in the dogs, despite his fears…

I had very much taken him for granted.

As I drove, I tried to figure out where I could possibly find him now. He rarely talked about himself, except in off-hand comments or when directly asked, so I had gathered up every bit of information I could and made an effort to remember. I had done that without realizing it, though it was useful now.

I combed through the fractured memories of our talks, digging up the names of places he had mentioned. The first one I remembered was Brighton Park, across the street from the local golf course. Brighton was small, but packed with interest, because it had several large gardens which the Red Bluff City Beautification Club — a subset of the regular park maintenance division, composed only of volunteers — focused on year-round.

The gardens were always overflowing with seasonal flowers and decorative displays. Each year was different, as the club tried not to be too repetitive. Martin had mentioned really loving the gardens, eagerly anticipating the turn of the seasons so he could see the next design.

I drove to Brighton as fast as I could, hoping against hope that he would be there. As soon as I reached the park, I flipped on my brights, illuminating most of the pathways and garden displays.

The scenes this time resembled an idyllic porch. Wooden furniture in bright primary colors filled the garden plots, around which pots and planters of flowers were arranged. One display even included the door leading out to a faux porch, and an umbrella over a glass table strewn with viridian ivy vines.

No sign of Martin, though.

Thinking that he might just be out of the reach of my headlights, I got out of the truck and faced the park. "Martin?" I called. My voice echoed strangely amongst the trees. "Martin, if you're out here, I need to talk to you."

No response. My heart sank and I clenched my fists, trying to keep a grip on myself.

This was just one place. There were lots of other places he could be, and I was sure to find him somewhere.

I waited for another few moments, just in case he decided to come out of hiding, but there was nothing. My shoulders sagging, I gave up and got back into my truck.

I stopped by the Red Bluff Inn, his favorite bar, but a quick scan of the parking lot told me he wasn't there. If I had been him, I probably would have been in there getting drunk. He was smarter than me, though.

My hands were tight on the steering wheel as I went to the next location. Pet Central. The store was closed, and it was too late for it to be open even if all the animals hadn't been evacuated. Still, he loved that job, and I wouldn't have been surprised if he'd sought comfort in the presence of animals. Like me.

The entrances to Pet Central's parking lot were blocked off by traffic cones and an absurd amount of caution tape. Martin wasn't there.

I went to Walmart, perusing the parking lot in search for his vehicle. I saw nothing, though by now I was beginning to second-guess myself. He could have left his car at an acquaintance's house; he could be anywhere at this point.

I headed inside the store, which was quiet and somehow eerie without the usual annoyance of too many customers. The few workers I saw looked as if they were true creatures of the night, sulking under the bright lights out on the floor, returning eagerly to the dimness of the back rooms.

No Martin.

I even approached a manager and had them send out a page over the intercom, asking Martin to come to the front desk if he was on the premises. He did not come, and I gave up after a few minutes. My spirits low and my options nearly exhausted after two hours of searching, I returned to my truck and moved on.

He was not at his favorite ice cream parlor, and he was not at the overlook near the Sacramento River.

I stood at the river with my hands on the railing, my head down. This was the last place I knew of to look for him. Wherever he was, he had successfully eluded my grasp.

Maybe that's for the best. I ruined it. Why should I get a second chance at this?

My constant giving up had done this. Instead of chasing after the opportunity presented to me, I had taken the easy way out. I was a poor idiot of a bastard, doomed to continued failure. I'd decided too late to get some sense of perseverance.

Martin had probably found somewhere to spend the night, despite his insistence that he had nowhere to go. Desperate people could do desperate things.

At that thought, a horrific idea formed. I clutched at the railing at the overlook, the sharp grit of rust biting into my palms. Suppose Martin had gone home to his parents, leaving this life behind?

I knew some of his history of them, and a bit about them in particular, but I didn't know where they lived or how to find them. I did have those resources at my disposal, being a man with close ties to the police department, but it wouldn't be worth it.

If he had gone home, there was nothing I could do. That was it.

I trembled, my shoulders shaking, and stared down at the surface of the river, watching the stars ripple as they were reflected on the water. I'd fucked up. I'd fucked up, and I could not come back from it this time. I'd best go home and start over, pretend I'd never met him.

Home.

Why did that word stick with me so strangely? My home; Martin's home. Something seemed wrong, and I couldn't quite figure out what it was.

"Martin went home," I said out loud, my voice flat and empty. "Martin went home?"

His parents' house would not be home to him. It was a place he'd escaped from, a cage from which he'd freed himself. He wouldn't ever go back.

He would have gone *home*. To his own fucking house, which I hadn't checked, because I was a fucking moron. His neighborhood was still off-limits, and no one was allowed through.

Except he knew me. He could put my name to use, and those idiots would let him pass, because they thought highly of me for some stupid reason.

I was running before I even knew what I was doing, rushing back the way I had come. Tossing myself into the truck, I started up the engine and backed out onto the street without looking. A car beeped behind me, and I heard the squeal of brakes.

Some young couple come to kiss at a romantic, moonlit spot. I didn't care. I slammed the gear into drive and my reliable truck, always so smooth and steady, bucked and jittered before catching.

I drove through the streets of Red Bluff like a man who was convinced he could fly, sending gravel spraying everywhere at every turn. It was a miracle no police officer stopped me, especially when I came closer to the evacuated neighborhoods. There should have been cops crawling all over this place.

I saw none.

If I'd been an upset man, seeking refuge from my own bad feelings, I would have had the easiest time getting in.

Even with the air conditioning on, the temperature rose as I came nearer the fire. I started to sweat, my palms and face going clammy. Droplets beaded on my forehead, stinging my eyes as they fell.

I saw the red blaze in the distance, the flashing lights of the firetrucks as my brothers continued the effort in my absence. Smoke blocked out the stars, the moon.

When I came to the evacuated neighborhoods, it seemed to me as if I had gone back in time, to some primitive age when even the sky wasn't fully formed yet. Certainly there wasn't electricity, or society. The empty houses were like monoliths, dedicated to some god who was no longer around.

Pushing the morbid thoughts away, I drove as fast as I dared and finally came to Martin's street. As I pulled onto the road, I saw a flash of metal down at the far end, where there shouldn't have been anything at all.

A car.

Martin's car.

My heart jumped into my throat, and I was sweating in earnest from a combination of fear and anticipation. My mind went blank; I almost panicked as I realized I hadn't actually prepared what I was going to say to him.

Then that brief panic was knocked out of my mind and replaced by true terror. I hadn't noticed up until now, because I was so focused on other things, but my throat hurt and my eyes were stinging for an entirely different reason besides sweat getting into them. The stench of smoke filled every rapid breath I took.

Goddammit, Martin. How could you come out here? Why couldn't you go drinking like a regular guy?

He was not a regular guy. He was one of a kind, and I needed to tell him that. I only hoped it wouldn't be too late.

Once I reached the edge of his tiny yard, I figured that was close enough and slammed on the brakes. I already had my seatbelt off, and momentum carried me hard against the steering wheel, almost onto the dashboard. Pushing myself away with my hands on the hot windshield, I grabbed for the door and fell out onto the street.

I hit the ground running and raced up to the front door. The knob twisted under my hand and I threw the door open, dashing inside.

The interior of the house was dark. No lights had been turned on, and I didn't have my headlights to guide my way. Squinting, I pushed my hand out in front of me and tried to feel around for a light switch.

"Martin?" I yelled. The air was so hot, so oppressive — what little of it there was. Each breath was three parts smoke, one part oxygen. I coughed to try and ease the burning in my throat, but giving in to the urge had only made things worse.

I coughed again, the irritation morphing into pain. "Martin?"

Finally finding the light switch, I flipped it. The lights flickered on and I blinked hard to try and adjust to the … brightness?

No. The lights hardly made a difference. Outside, the smoke had had a chance to dissipate. Inside, smoke could not escape, and it built and built in opacity, turning the interior of the house filmy. Everything was swathed in gray.

My mouth tasted like I'd been sucking on a lit birthday candle.

"Martin?" I looked around the living room, searching for him. No sign of recent habitation, as far as I could tell.

On a whim, I ran in the direction of what I hoped was a bedroom. A few doorways at the end of a hall. I shoved one open, discovered a bathroom. My reflection was a haunted, ghoulish thing.

I turned to the next door and tried to open it. The knob jiggled, stayed in position. Locked.

He's in there.

Luckily, I had been trained for these eventualities.

I took a few steps back, into the bathroom, until my calves touched the tub. Digging my feet in, I ran at the door and thrust my shoulder at the hinges.

People always went for the knob and the lock itself, not understanding they were focusing on metal and mechanism. The hinges were the weaker part of the door. You didn't need to break them. All you had to do was damage the wood connected to them.

There was a tremendous cracking sound as I rebounded from the door, my shoulder pounding with pain. Hot white lights flashed behind my eyelids. Gritting my teeth, I backed up again and threw myself into another tackle.

Wood screamed as it splintered, and I collapsed through the doorway, tripping over the door. I couldn't catch myself and landed hard on my side.

Pain jabbed at me, a stinging that reminded me of tripping on the blacktop at recess when I was a kid, scraping the flesh off my palms as I tried to catch myself. Only this was about five times worse.

I hardly gave a fuck about the pain, and it was soon enough an afterthought, swallowed up by adrenaline pumping through my system. I picked myself up and as I did so, I caught sight of someone lying on the bed.

Martin's face was blue, his eyes closed.

"Fuck!"

Stumbling, tripping over the broken door, I collapsed against the bed and flung my arm out to slap Martin across the face. It would have been more eloquent to check his pulse, but I didn't have time for finesse.

Martin flinched from the pain, his eyelids fluttering. A soft sound escaped from between his lips, and then he sank back into unconsciousness.

He was alive.

I grabbed him in my arms and ran out of the house, wheezing. Waiting out here for an ambulance to come would be counterproductive, so I just threw Martin into the back seat and drove as fast as I could with the air-conditioning on full blast. I had to hope that a constant influx of cold, fresh air would help him until we reached the hospital.

Before we were even halfway there, I saw a flash of lights behind me. My heart, which had already taken some massive abuse tonight, skipped in my chest. A cop. Of course.

Well, fuck him. I had better places to be. If he wanted to follow me all the way to the hospital, I wasn't going to stop him.

The cop tailed me, his siren blazing. He shouted over his speakers, not that I could hear anything he said. Then, suddenly, as I reached the hospital, the cop turned off his lights and siren and went off in a different direction.

I could only wonder at his sudden disinterest. Had he realized that I had an emergency situation and could be excused for speeding, or had he called in my plate number and learned who I was? A combination of both?

It didn't matter. Only Martin did.

I parked in front of the ER, grabbed him against my chest, and ran inside as fast as I could. I felt his heart beating, weak and fragile against mine.

Please let him be okay. Please let me have this second chance. I will do anything.

Chapter 16 - Martin

The last memory I had was of drifting down into a warm sea, the taste of salt on my lips. Breathing hadn't been necessary, and my awareness of that had grown shallow before disappearing altogether.

I didn't know when things had changed, or how. Recollection was hazy. I dreamed/remembered/imagined a sharp pain, followed by a sensation of speed.

My body was running without me. Or maybe something was moving me. I wasn't sure.

Voices. One low and gruff and familiar, making me want to smile. The other voices I hadn't ever heard them before. There sure were a lot of them.

After that, not much except sleep.

I wasn't quite sure when sleep became consciousness. The darkness behind my eyelids melted into a harsh whiteness that hurt me, making me blink a lot.

I tried to focus, although the whiteness didn't seem to want to fade. I grunted, a little displeased. Whatever the hell this was, I wasn't enjoying it.

My grunt didn't make a sound, which was weird.

Eventually, I realized the reason why I was having such a hard time seeing was because there was a row of lights above me. The lights were white against a stark white ceiling, which struck me as kind of stupid. Even the walls were white. So incredibly boring. Lance at least had his walls painted a pleasant beige-tan color.

Lance.

I wasn't in his house. I wasn't in my house, either. So where…?

A suspicion bubbled up in the back of my mind. Turning my head, I looked around to see if I could confirm it. I lay in a white bed in a white room, which had white furniture and blank walls. The lights were white.

On either side of me were machines, chrome-colored, from which came faint purring sounds and the occasional beep. Wires led from the machines, attached to me in different places. A few of the wires ended in electrodes, which were stuck to my chest.

Another of the wires was an IV, which meant there was a needle stuck in my skin. I said, "Ugh," but not much sound happened.

The last wire turned out not to be a wire at all, but a clear plastic tube that wove its way up onto the bed, across my shoulder, and to my face. I could feel the pressure of something on my mouth and nose now, though I hadn't been aware of it before because I wasn't paying attention.

A mask?

Had something happened to me? I started to breathe a little shallower, worry niggling at me, like worms wriggling through soil. The last thing I really remembered was going home and thinking about how good it felt to lie down in bed, how tired I had been. I'd closed my eyes for only a moment, and now I was here.

A machine to my left let out a beep which was different-sounding from the rest. I looked up, trying to figure out what the hell that was about. I didn't know enough about hospitals to know what any of this meant.

And that was when I saw him.

I hadn't noticed him before because I hadn't been looking for him. Even if I had been, he kind of blended into the background.

Lance.

He wore a white hospital gown, sitting in one of the chairs on the other side of the room. He had his head leaned back against the wall, his eyes closed.

"Lance?" I said.

My voice still made no sound, muffled by the damnable mask. Frustrated, I grabbed the mask with the arm that wasn't impaled by an IV needle and yanked it away from my mouth. "Lance!"

He sat up in one sudden movement, like a piston pumping, and looked around as if he was trying to reorient himself. His eyes landed on me and his entire face lit up.

"Martin!" he cried out and crossed over to my side in a single leap. "What are you doing, you idiot? Put your mask back on!"

Before I could do anything, Lance grabbed the mask and pushed it up into place again. The influx of fresh air made me dizzy, and I had to close my eyes to combat the sensation.

When I opened my eyes again, an unfamiliar woman stood over me. She was, of course, dressed in white. She smiled when she noticed me looking at her, and lifted her hand to flutter her fingers at me, a teasing little wave.

"Look who's awake," she said. She had a bit of an Indian accent and, now that I was looking for it, I noticed the darker cast to her skin. The harsh lights mellowed the color.

"Do you know who you are?"

"Martin Fleming," I answered. I could still barely hear myself, and the mask was pushing on my nose, making me sound nasally. "I'm in the hospital?"

"Correct," she said. "I'm Dr. Patel. You've been unconscious for two years."

I stared at her, feeling all the blood drain from my face. The machine at my side let out another of those odd, startled little beeps.

Two years?

Suddenly, Dr. Patel laughed and patted the back of my hand. "Oh, dear. Calm down. It was just a joke. It's only been a few hours. Don't worry."

I stared at her, feeling like things didn't make much sense right now. "I want to be mad at you," I said. "But I'm too busy being relieved that I haven't been in a coma for two years."

Dr. Patel smiled and patted my hand again. "Good. Then, my strategy worked."

Damn, I think I like her.

"Do you remember what happened, Martin?" As she awaited my answer, Dr. Patel started checking me over. It was difficult to concentrate when she was hovering around me, and I was thinking about Lance, so it took me a minute.

"I went back home," I recalled. "And then I … went to sleep."

"Technically, you passed out. Would you take a deep breath, please?" Dr. Patel removed the mask from my face and pressed her stethoscope against my skin.

The fierce cold definitely helped me take that deep breath. After listening, Dr. Petal leaned back and let her stethoscope dangle around her neck. "Well, you sound much better than when you first arrived. You have a nice set of young, healthy lungs."

By now, I was starting to put things together. "I passed out from smoke inhalation?"

"Yes, you did. You're very lucky that your friend Lance found you and pulled you out. It was a very close thing. Had you been in your home much longer, this would be a much less pleasing outcome."

Dr. Patel paused. "How would you rate your pain, and where?"

Did I hurt? "My throat is sore," I said. "And my head kind of hurts."

"Nothing else?"

"Nothing else. And it's not too bad."

"That's very good, and is to be expected. Starving your brain of the air it needs is bound to be a little painful. You realize how foolish your actions were, don't you?"

Shame prickled at me, and I looked away. "Yeah."

I had just been so frustrated, so overwhelmed, and I had followed Quincy's idyllic advice without really considering the consequences of what I was doing. I'd gone home, like a moron and it nearly killed me. The only reason it hadn't was because of...

"Lance," I said out loud. I looked around, and couldn't see him in the room. "Is he here?"

"We sent him back to his own room because he violated our agreement." Dr. Patel's deep brown eyes glimmered with a mixture of amusement and exasperation. "We told him he could stay in here if he behaved himself. He was too excitable, and we had to send him back.

"You can see him again shortly, when we release you. I just need to examine you a little further."

It certainly sounded like Lance, to be incapable of doing what someone told him. I started to laugh, and then I realized what else she had said. "Hold on. His own room?"

My pulse started to race, a rushing like ocean waves in my ears. He had been wearing a hospital gown. What the hell had happened to him?

My stupid decision to run home instead of sticking around to talk things out had hurt him. I was never going to forgive myself for that.

Somehow, I made it through the rest of the examination, and Dr. Patel announced me to be startlingly healthy after the amount of smoke I'd inhaled. She prescribed bed rest, little physical activity for the next couple of days, and a round of aspirin for my headache.

That, and maybe a little tea with honey, would be all I needed to recover. The same couldn't be said for Lance.

As soon as I was released and dressed again in my own clothes, I demanded to be taken to his room. I pushed my way in without knocking and looked around for him.

He sat on the edge of his hospital bed, still wearing that hideous white gown. It was untied at the back and had slipped forward on his shoulders, enough for me to be able to see swathes of white bandages covering his ribs.

Lifting his head from his hand, Lance saw me standing in the doorway and his face lit up again. My own face burned, and I could hardly stand to look at him. I didn't deserve that kind of attention from him. I didn't deserve to have him be happy to see me.

"You're up and walking! That's great!" Lance started to get to his feet, supporting himself against the wall and grimacing.

"What happened to you?" I whispered. My legs trembled, my knees on the verge of giving out. "What did I do to you?"

Lance's eyes darkened, and that somehow hurt less than having him be happy to see me. It was more what I deserved to see from him. "You didn't do anything to me. Don't be stupid. Least you could do is look happy to see the guy who saved your life."

"My life isn't worth you being hurt!"

"I say otherwise, so you have to deal with that." Lance finally got to his feet. Reaching around, he tore the gown off the rest of the way and stood naked before me. The glory of his image was ruined by those bandages.

"Look. It's not that bad, okay? I'd already be out of here, but I pulled some stitches back in your room when I saw you were awake. My fault, not yours. So shut up about that 'your life isn't worth it' shit."

I desperately wanted to believe him. I couldn't. Not yet. "How did you get hurt?"

"How? I'll tell you how. I broke down your bedroom door, and then I tripped and fell right on top of the broken, pointy parts. I needed some stitches. Nothing to it."

"That sounds like a whole lot of something," I said. My voice was as weak as my wobbly legs. "How could you even bother to do something like that for me?"

Lance strode across the small room and wrapped his arms around me. I felt his soft cock against my leg, stiffening slightly in an instinctive way. His chin rested on top of my head, holding me in place against him. "Shut up," he growled. "And listen to me. I made a mistake. We both did."

Does that mean...

Something like hope, wretched in its blind tenacity, reared its head inside me. I was powerless to stop myself from pressing closer to him, shutting my eyes tight to enjoy the feel of his solid body supporting mine.

It shouldn't have been this way. He was injured, and yet he was still being the strong one.

"I'm not strong," Lance said, like he'd read my thoughts. "I'm pretty damn stupid. I'm weak. I didn't realize how much I wanted you until I almost lost you."

I pulled in a quick breath, held it. He couldn't possibly mean that. Could he?

His arms tightened around me, like he'd sensed my reaction. "I have a lot of things to tell you once we get home.

"Yeah, you heard me right. You're coming home with me again. And if you ever want to leave my house again, for anything, I'm going to follow you the whole way."

I laughed and buried my face in Lance's chest. He smelled of smoke, of sweat, of man.

His fingers ruffled in my hair and then his stubbled cheek was on mine. I rested my head against his, then turned and kissed him.

He settled his lips firmly on mine and kissed me back. It was different from any other time we had kissed so far. He seemed to be making a promise to me, instead of trying to claim me.

Someone coughed behind us. I spun around and a nurse stood there, her arms folded, and a stern look on her face. Her eyes betrayed her amusement, however. They twinkled.

"Since you're already undressed, Mr. Williams, I think now would be a good time to check you over again one last time. If you haven't busted another stitch, we'll probably let you get out of here."

Lance blushed. It was the first time I'd ever seen him blush, and it struck me like a lightning bolt that he was cute.

This huge, gruff man doted on his dogs like they were babies and blushed when tiny nurses teased him.

I was so glad he had come and saved me, if only for the chance to experience this moment.

I went out to wait in the hall. A few minutes after that, Lance emerged, fully-dressed. He checked himself out of the hospital, and then held out his hand for me. "Let's go home," he said.

I stared at his hand, too surprised to accept.

Lance grabbed my hand in his and pulled me along behind him in the direction of his truck. His fingers wrapped around mine so easily. It felt so good to just walk along at his side, our hips occasionally brushing together. Pale dawn light surrounded us, making the experience seem ethereal and dreamlike.

We didn't talk during the ride home. I mostly just focused on the way my fingers tingled, like my skin was searching for him even after he'd let go of me.

Once we were back at his house, he tended to the dogs and then headed into the kitchen. I followed him and helped make coffee. While that was brewing, we ate cake.

I didn't comment on the fact that there had already been a piece sliced and placed on a plate, with only a single bite taken. The story there was clear enough.

As soon as we both had coffee, Lance sighed and looked over at me. His eyes were bright and more blue than green. They shimmered like twin gemstones. I couldn't look away, and had to force myself to even concentrate on what he was saying.

"I didn't mean to hurt you before, when I said no to a date."

"It's okay," I said, but he cut me off, shaking his head.

"It wasn't okay. I acted like a fool without really thinking." He grimaced, true regret obvious on his face.

"I acted like I would have in the past, instead of acting how I should have. I didn't want to admit to myself that you … that maybe you meant more to me than I wanted."

My mouth went dry. I clutched my coffee mug, hardly daring to believe what he was hinting at.

"I'm not used to people thinking about me the way that you do. I keep distance. Especially now.

"I have a lot of secrets. You have no idea how scared I am that you'll hate me." His strong voice trembled, and I saw that he, too, was gripping his mug for dear life.

It seemed to be my turn to talk. "Lance, I asked you for a date because I want to be the person you come to. It's more than just stress relief now. Don't you feel that?

"I want it because it's you. Because of the way you make me feel, and the way I feel when we spend time together. This hasn't ever happened to me before, and I want more of it."

Lance nodded. I thought he might reach out to me and that we would cuddle, since this felt like a natural end to the conversation for me. We'd affirmed our feelings for one another. What else was left for us to do?

But it seemed like he wasn't done yet.

"One of the reasons I'm scared to get closer to you is because of my secrets. Martin, they aren't good."

I really, really hated to see him looking like this, so very unlike himself. I tilted my head, watching him. "Lance, I've been all over your house. I've spent hours and hours with you. Talking to you.

"You've never once said or done anything secretive. Whatever it is, it can't be as bad as you think."

He smiled, and it was more like a grimace. "It's worse than you think. I don't know how to say this, so I'll just go ahead and get it out there. I'm an arsonist."

I looked at Lance, puzzled. Arsonist? "You set fires? I don't think that's what you meant to say. What do you mean?"

He was a firefighter, for crying out loud. This was going to be just a funny mistake. He had used the wrong word.

Kind of an interesting word to get mixed up on, though. It was a little too coincidental to be an actual coincidence.

Suspicion formed in the back of my brain. It couldn't really be, could it? There was no way.

The look Lance gave me said yes way. He believed what he was saying. He *knew* what he was saying, and he had used the right word. His guilty conviction was staring me right in the face.

"What?" I whispered. The world seemed to tilt around me, the bottom dropping out of my stomach.

Lance shoved his coffee mug away and gripped the table. His shoulders heaved. "I'm an arsonist, Martin. I started this fire, the one that forced you out of your home. The one that's affected dozens, hundreds of lives.

"It's my fault. I did it. And I started the fire before this one, and the one before that. And the one before that. They've all been my doing."

Vertigo washed over me. I felt like I was stuck in the middle of a whirlpool, being spun around endlessly until I lost my strength and drowned. "But, that can't be right," I sputtered. "Red Bluff hasn't had a fire like this, ever. You can't start something that hasn't happened."

He looked at me with something like pity in his eyes. He really wanted me to believe this charade of his. "The fires are supposed to be small. That way, we can put them out and prove that we're still useful, so our budget won't be cut. If I create work for us, work we can easily do, then I make sure of that."

"Your budget won't be cut?" Amidst my confusion, anger started to rise. Whether this was a charade or the truth, I was mad about it.

If he was lying to me, I was mad. If he was telling the truth, I was furious. Why the fuck would he do something like this? Start fires? For money?

Lance shuddered. His breath came faster and I saw his pulse beat rapidly at the hollow of his throat. "Yeah. That's what it's all about.

"The fire department, the police force, the town maintenance teams. We're all going to have our budgets cut. The vote hasn't been officially cast yet, but we all know it's set in stone.

"Chief Patrick devised a plan. If we could prove that we're still needed, just as much as always, we wouldn't get a budget cut. And neither would the police, because they have to show up at the site of every fire to check things out. And the town maintenance teams would have their work cut out for them restoring the damage. We would all benefit. No budget cuts, no jobs lost."

All of this made a terrible sort of sense, and that was why I believed it.

This man I had come to admire so much was an arsonist. Even if he believed it was for a good cause, it was still so wrong that there was no way I could forgive it. Never.

I almost died because I was depressed over you? If only I'd known this sooner.

"Don't look at me like that," Lance whispered, pleading. "I didn't have a choice."

"What do you mean, you didn't have a choice? You had every choice!"

"No! Let me tell you everything, okay? And then you can decide to hate me."

I crossed my arms and stared at him, waiting. He must have seen my anger, because he wouldn't look me in the eyes anymore.

"Chief Patrick blackmailed me. He told me that this was a job for me, that he didn't trust anyone else to keep their mouth shut. He said if I didn't do this, then he would do it himself, and blame it all on me anyway.

"He'd fabricate the books so it looked like I had been stealing money, too. He'd put the dogs down. I had to do it."

"Why would he pick you?" I demanded.

"Because I'm a fucking pushover!" Lance snapped. He stood up and slammed his hands down on the table, knocking over his coffee cup. "I want things to be easy, and the easiest thing to do is just fucking give up.

"I gave up on myself. I gave up on you. I gave up on the family farm business. I moved states away so I wouldn't have anything to do with that life anymore, because I fucked up. Do you understand now?"

Now that he had put everything out in the open for me, I could see it all so clearly. Except there was still something that didn't quite make sense. "You haven't given up on the dogs."

"No," Lance agreed. He pushed his hands through his hair, making it stick up in spikes. Then he grimaced, and placed one hand over his injured side.

"I haven't ever. I don't know why. All I know is that I've been using them as an excuse, telling myself that if I let Patrick use this against me and have me arrested, I'll never have the dogs in the way I want.

"All my efforts will have been for nothing. It's like they're the only things that matter. Or, it was like that, anyway. Until you came along. And now I don't know what to do with myself."

He clearly felt awful, to the point where it was causing him physical pain. After hearing all his reasons for his actions, there was no way I could stay angry with him. Well, maybe a little.

But I was more angry at this Chief Patrick person. He couldn't have come up with a legal way to solve the problem? He'd picked on someone he knew would listen to him. Someone who was a real softie on the inside.

I stood up from my seat and went around the table to Lance, avoiding the puddle of hot coffee. I wrapped my arms around him and hugged him tightly, just like he had hugged me not all that long ago. Stroking his hair, holding his rigid form, I whispered, "It's okay."

"No, it isn't." Lance trembled, an earthquake in my arms. His skin was cold, covered in goosebumps.

"It will be. Because you're never, ever going to start another fire."

Lance lifted his head and turned to look at me. He looked so hopeful that I felt my heart twist. The last of the anger I had aimed towards him disappeared. "Never," he echoed. "I never will. Ever."

"You have to promise."

"I promise!"

"And you have to mean it," I said firmly. "You really have to mean it. I understand everything you've said, but the problem is only going to get worse the more you keep giving in. So no more."

Lance turned fully in my arms to face me. He clutched at me, pressing our bodies together. His heartbeat was loud enough for both of us. "Does this mean that we're okay?"

"Well, I still want to be with you," I said, and I meant it. Learning his secrets had changed my perception of him, not my opinions. Nothing could make me deny how I felt towards him. "I want to trust you. I want to see where we can go. Don't you?"

I held my breath, waiting. There was always a chance that my knowledge of his secrets would cause him to shy away from me, even more than before. There wouldn't be any point in pursuing him after that. Like an injured animal, he would only flee from me.

Lance lowered his head until our foreheads touched. He looked deeply into my eyes, making it difficult to focus on anything else but him. "I want to stick with you. I don't want to give up anymore."

That was more than good enough for me.

Leaning into him, I pressed my lips to his. Our mouths melded, and a tide of light, happy tingles danced throughout my body. I clutched at his shoulders, standing on my toes to settle my lips more firmly on his.

Lance tilted his head back and looked at me. "Will you go on a date with me?"

"No," I said. Before his disappointed look could get any worse, I continued. "Not until your side feels better. I'd hate to have to end our date early because I have to take you to the hospital."

He scoffed, looking indignant. The haughty expression didn't work very well with his strong features, and I laughed, which made him look even more offended. "I feel fine, dammit. I'll prove it to you."

"Prove it how?"

Lance picked me up in his arms, startling me. I yelped and clutched at him with my arms and legs, trying to support myself. His stubble rasped on my cheek as he nuzzled his face on mine, and then he kissed me again, and I had to fight to keep from going limp.

Slow, lazy heat suffused my body. My toes curled.

"Convinced yet?" he whispered, his breath warm on my neck.

His erection pushed against me, hot and ready for me. Arching my back, I ground on him and was delighted to hear him gasp.

"I think I need a little more proof," I said.

He kissed me again, briefly but intensely, his lips claiming mine for a rough instant. Then he strode out of the kitchen with me in his arms, through the living room, heading for his bedroom.

Fear sliced through my lust for him. I held him tighter with my legs, trying to propel myself higher up his body. "Lance, the dogs!"

"I got you," he said, his voice deep and soothing. He slid his arm underneath my ass to support me while opening the bedroom door. The dogs lay cuddled up on the floor. They must have fallen asleep while playing together, because they both had their mouths wrapped around a blue tug toy.

"Spot, Dottie. Wake up."

At the sound of their master's voice, the two dogs awoke and jumped up. They sprang for him, and I tucked my head against his neck, a whimper lodging in my throat. Spotting me, they both came crashing to a halt right in front of us. Their tails wagged, uncertain.

From my vantage point, I could look right into their eyes. So warm, so brown. So intelligent and eager to please. They seemed almost human.

Lance stepped out of the doorway. "Out, both of you," he said.

The dogs trotted through the door. I tensed up as they passed by, relaxing when they were gone.

Lance shut the door. We had the room all to ourselves now.

Chapter 17 - Lance

I took Martin over to my bed and set him down, then leaned my body over his and pressed my lips to his. He tasted sweet, like coffee and cake, and I sank against him to get more of him.

My lips claimed his, devouring them. I tugged on his lower lip, biting at it. I teased him with my tongue, little flicks to get him chasing after me, only to press forward and take him again harder than before.

His lips were parted, his breathing deep and fast. Little moans escaped his throat, each one causing my level of desire to rise by another notch.

I held his hips and slid up onto the bed over him, pushing him down onto his back. He wrapped his legs around me, and the feel of our bodies tangling together made me get a little breathless.

I held him harder, pressing fierce kisses against his lips over and over. I thrust my tongue into his mouth and he eagerly gave me entrance, his tongue hungry to meet mine.

Our tongues played between us, mimicking sex, but it wasn't enough just to pretend. I wanted more.

Grinding my hips on his, I trailed a kiss down his cheek, to his chin, and to his throat. I kissed his racing pulse, danced my lips over to his shoulder, and nibbled and sucked at his skin until he squirmed and tugged at my hair for me to stop. I let him feel my teeth, a growl rising in my throat. A warning that he belonged to me, and I would do what I wanted to him.

Unbelievably, Martin growled back. I felt, more than heard, the rumble in his chest. Looking up into his eyes, I saw the amusement and joy written on his features. I nuzzled my nose on his and rubbed our lips together. "You think you're a tough guy, huh?" I growled.

In answer, Martin dug his nails into my back and scratched me. I was still wearing a shirt, so I didn't feel much besides his fingers moving down my back.

I wanted to feel more. I wanted him to be rough with me. I wanted him to do whatever the fuck he wanted.

I kissed him again and gave him another nuzzle, then pushed him down into the bed. He gasped and arched underneath me, his dick searching desperately for mine.

Rising up onto my knees over his body, I stripped off my shirt and tossed it to the side. Martin's eyes widened when he saw me, their dark color lightening with appreciation. I could see myself reflected in them like a mirror.

The bandages wrapped around my abdomen kind of ruined the image, but whatever. I healed fast. They'd be gone soon.

"You're so nice," Martin sighed.

I laughed. "Nice? That's the best word you can come up with, in the middle of sex?"

"It feels weird to call you handsome. That doesn't describe you well enough."

"What about godly?" I teased, tearing my pants off at the same time.

Martin let out a long, satisfied sigh. "I know you're joking, but that about does it."

Chuckling, I pulled my cock out of my underwear for him to see. I was fully erect, lusting for his body. My shaft was long and thick, the peak of male pleasure.

Martin knew that too, having done this with me before. However, he reacted like this was his first time seeing me. His nostrils flared, and his pupils dilated. His lips parted, like he was already imagining having me inside him.

Spying the bulge under his own clothes, I slid my hand down his pants and gripped him. He gasped, arching his back and pushing against my fingers. I pressed the flat of my hand against his dick, rubbing him. He tossed his head back and gasped again.

"You like that?" I rumbled. "You want more of that?"

"Don't tease me," he begged, but of course that meant I was now obligated to do so.

I rubbed him again, and his entire body moved to follow the motion of my hand. He trembled, muscles quivering.

Leaning over him with my hand still pushed against him, I kissed him and growled against his lips.

All the other times I'd fucked someone, I'd never paired with a person well enough to feel like this while just playing around. Martin made me feel like a true alpha male. He was an omega through and through, not just in the shape of his body, but in the way he made me feel.

How the hell could I ever have doubted this?

I slid my hands up underneath Martin's shirt and tossed it aside. I did the same for his pants and underwear, my every movement growing rougher and more excited as his body was revealed to me again. His slender shape excited me, made me pound for him.

I kissed his compact shoulders, the soft hollow of his throat, trailing my tongue down his chest to the thin thatch of golden hairs between his pecs. Seeking out his nipple, I sucked on one while rasping my thumb over the other. They went erect at my attention, and I toyed with them, flicking them gently with my tongue, my finger.

Moaning, Martin clutched at me. His legs around me, he bucked against me with need. I felt that need echoed in every fiber of my being. It was carved into my bones, an essential part of me.

I was made for him. That much was clear now.

I danced more kisses over his body, down to the apex of his thighs. More golden hair, more crinkly than it was fine. The texture was exciting on my sensitive lips, and I slid my mouth through the patch until I found what I had been aiming for all this time.

The shaft of his dick was covered in soft skin, glorious to touch. I slid my lips up his length, admiring his shape and girth. For a little guy, he had a hell of a lot going on down here.

I felt each centimeter of his texture intimately. His veins, his rigidness, his softness. His head was burning hot and red for me, like a flame in and of itself. It was my job as a firefighter to extinguish that flame, and so I did what was naturally the best course of action. After all, I always knew what to do.

I wrapped my mouth around his tip and sucked.

I meant to bring him even higher by teasing him, but my plan backfired on me. All my attention to his body, combined with this final act, sent him over the edge. His body jerked and his dick jumped, and I only had half a second to move out of the way as he came.

I wasn't above putting my mouth on him to pleasure him, unlike a lot of alpha guys, but I wasn't a swallower. Watching him was enough. His eyes were squeezed shut tight, and his mouth was open, releasing tremulous gasps of breath.

Slowly, he sagged back down onto the mattress. He'd had his turn. Now it was mine.

Ignoring the resulting pain in my side from my stupid injuries, I reached over and grabbed my lube. While Martin recovered, I slathered lube all over my pounding cock, until I was dripping with my own readiness. Pulses of desire shivered through my loins, guiding me.

I followed their influence and moved closer to him until I was pressed against his ass opening. He was loose in his relaxation after orgasm, and I slid inside with the slightest push.

Martin revived in an instant. He grabbed for me and tilted his hips up to give me better access to his depths.

I pushed myself deeper inside him, careful to hold back so I wouldn't hurt him. He was still too new to this for me to jump on him right away.

As before, being inside him was like being in a different world composed of pleasure. My awareness of my surroundings narrowed down until it was only him and me. Just the two of us. All alone, for us to do whatever we wished.

All alone, for me to do whatever I wanted.

Bracing myself with a hand on either side of his body, I sank myself deeper inside him. He trembled, tightening and loosening around me in pulses as his muscles shifted to accommodate for me.

Whenever he grabbed me like that, I had to gasp at how glorious it was. It was like I was flying, and he was the breeze pushing me higher and higher, into the sky and beyond, into space.

Some of my control slipped. I thrust deeper into Martin, shoving his body with the movement. He cried out and gripped me, and I tried to stop, thinking I had hurt him. Then I realized he was pulling on me, asking me to keep going, to give him another one.

I was only too glad to answer, and I let some of the wild animal inside me come out, thrusting inside him again. I hit my limit, my hips flush against his ass cheeks. He started grinding on me, his body bucking.

I followed his movements, thrusting with him. Slowly at first, matching his rhythm. In and out, as easy as pie, enjoying the sensation of his inner ridges and textures gliding over me.

Then I picked up the pace. Faster now, rushing him, forcing him to hurry to keep up. I wasn't worried, because his face was the face of a man enjoying the best ride of his life. He let out soft cries and yelps of pleasure, then picked up speed on his own.

Grinning, I leaned over him and kissed his throat, biting at him with my lips while giving him everything I had to offer. The last of my control gone, I rode him. I claimed him.

Lifting my hips, I pulled almost all the way out before fucking back inside him. Underneath me, he trembled and writhed, while matching me every step of the way.

We were connected. Our hearts pounded together, and we breathed in the same ragged way. Two halves of the same whole, we chased each other higher and higher into that sky in the search for bliss.

A massive wave of heat rocked through my body, a supernova exploding somewhere. I yelled out as I felt myself buoyed on the blast, ceasing to exist in thought. I was aware of nothing as I came.

Nothing but Martin and his body, the sounds he made, the heat on my stomach as he orgasmed for a second time.

I sagged on top of him, my eyes closed. Lights played behind my eyelids, and I was replete.

But, as anyone who's ever fucked knows, the aftermath doesn't last. The pleasure drained from me, leaving me feeling hollow. Lacking adrenaline, I quivered, weakened.

Martin shifted beneath me. I rolled off to free him from my weight, expecting him to head off now that we were done.

After all, a good romp or not, I was still a filthy lawbreaker who had ruined his life.

Instead of leaving, Martin tucked himself against my body and laid his cheek on my chest. I held him, some of that empty space inside me was filled up by his presence.

I won't give up on you this time, I promised silently.

But that wasn't going to be enough. I closed my eyes and swore another solemn vow.

I won't give up on myself, either.

That felt better, and I allowed myself to finally relax, drifting into sleep. It was the best sleep I had had for the longest time, and not in the least part because of the warm presence lingering at the edge of my dreams.

Chapter 18 - Martin

Sex was great. Like, really, really great. Sometimes, a blow job or a hand job just felt kind of lacking. There was this place deep inside me that begged for attention during those times, a place that couldn't be reached.

When Lance was inside me, his every thrust caused him to hit that seat of pleasure. My orgasms were so much more intense because they came from deeper inside me, instead of coming from the surface. And the high that followed made me feel like I was walking on clouds … even if my ass ached a little.

On the other hand, Lance always seemed to come down a little after orgasm. Like he had to recharge. Maybe it was rougher on the giver than the receiver.

Either way, there was nothing I liked more than to cuddle up with him and listen to his heartbeat saying my name. Calling to me, slower and slower, until I fell asleep.

Lately, though, the need for sleep was never far away. I'd been feeling run down, like I was on the verge of getting sick. Each day seemed to get a tiny bit harder, plagued as I was by an illness that never fully arrived.

I even felt nauseous from time to time. It was never bad enough to take me down, but it was constant and noticeable.

A few weeks passed. The threat of the fire continued to lessen in measurable, controlled increments. I got to where I didn't really care about not being able to work.

Lance and I never did get to go on that date, but the time we spent together now always seemed to have a date-like quality to it. We held hands a lot, which was never going to get old, and sat close together at all times. We always had to be touching in some way, and that was fine with me.

I worked on my fear of Spot and Dottie. I didn't make huge strides, but I didn't really need to, because something was different. Maybe seeing Lance hold me meant something to them in their little doggy brains, because they seemed to have a new respect for me.

They no longer charged for Lance if I was anywhere near him, which meant I slowly grew comfortable having them in the room. I didn't touch them, or give them commands, or anything else, except be near them.

"Considering that you used to scream when you saw them," Lance teased me, "I think you aren't giving yourself enough credit."

I scowled at him and scooted away from him on the couch, regretting having said anything about it. At the same time, something deep inside me wondered if he might be right. Just before the fire, I'd been stared down by a chihuahua; now, I lounged in comfort in the presence of massive Dalmatians.

So maybe I was doing pretty okay. And that, of course, meant fate had to change things up right when I was comfortable.

A text lit up my phone screen later that some night. Not weird, but kind of unusual these days. Most of my communication had been with my boss and co-workers, discussing shifts and such. Lacking a job, there wasn't much to talk about anymore.

Picking up my phone, I saw who the text was from. Chris. My manager.

I swallowed hard, nervousness prickling at me. On the other side of the room, Dottie lifted her head and looked over at me with her ears pricked. She was sensing my fear, maybe hoping I'd let her do her job and accept comfort.

I couldn't deal with two stresses at once, though. I opened up the text and read the message.

It was short and to the point. Pet Central had been taken off the risk charts. A firefighter had performed an inspection of the building and cleared it as being okay for continued business.

Chris wanted me to come back to work tomorrow to help. We weren't going to have any animals for a few more days yet, since we had to schedule pickups to get them all back. Instead, we were going to be cleaning and stocking.

"Maybe I should quit," I muttered under my breath. My stomach churned in a slow, bitter way, too intense to be caused by just nerves. That weird almost-sickness again.

Lance looked over at me, his fingers twitching in surprise where they'd been resting on my thigh. "Quit what?" he asked, baffled.

"The store's opening up again tomorrow."

Before I could do anything else, Lance smiled for me. His handsomeness momentarily stole my breath away, making me forget what I'd been stressing over. "That's great! You've been wanting to get back to work."

Maybe I'd mentioned it a few times, but it had started to seem almost unreal, like it would never happen. "Why would you want to quit?" he said.

I dropped my phone on the floor. The dogs were trained to pick up dropped items, since having an extra helping "hand" in an emergency could be beneficial. I'd seen them fetch all sorts of things for Lance.

If he got naked, they'd grab his underwear and shove it into his hand. Drop a fork, they'd give it back and expect him to use it —despite the slobber.

My dropped phone caught their attention, though they made no move to act when they realized who they'd be dealing with. Their intense glances didn't bother me much.

"I kind of made a fool of myself last time, during the evacuation," I admitted. "How can I go back to work, knowing that they know? They'll be judging me the whole time."

Lance patted my shoulder, almost knocking me over. "What's more important to you? Them, or the animals?"

There was only one right answer to that question, so that put an end to the conversation. I did my best to get some good sleep that night and drove to work the next morning, still tired, trying to mull over the decision I had to make.

It seemed like everything in my life was changing. I could sit here and continue to let this part be the same as always, or I could try to change it, too.

Once again, there was really only one correct option, so I squared my shoulders and tried to pretend I was confident. I imagined the way Lance held himself, how he walked with his back straight and his chest forward, like he was always ready to meet a challenge if it came his way. Stepping out of my car, I lifted my chin, flung my shoulders back, and strode inside the store.

Chris stood just inside, his arms folded as he looked around. There were a few others already at work, armed with brooms and mops and buckets. The cleaning was under way, the sharp scent of chemicals vying with the lingering tang of smoke.

"Hi, Chris," I said, walking up to him.

He turned to face me and one of his eyebrows arched up. "You okay? You look really stiff."

So much for my go-getter posture. It hadn't done anything for me anyway, since I was still nervous as hell. "I'm okay. I need to talk to you about something."

His eyes went flat and guarded, shutting me out. I couldn't tell what he was thinking, although his reaction led me to believe I could make an educated guess. "We can always talk about anything at any time. However, today is not a good day for conversation. Maybe tomorrow."

"It needs to be today," I insisted. Tomorrow, I wouldn't have the balls for it.

Chris nodded. "If that's what you want. What is it?"

"The Junior Manager position is still open. I want to formally apply for an interview."

My voice shook on the last word. I tried to get ahold of myself. "I know my performance up until now has been lacking in some important areas.

"But during our break, I've been working on my flaws. I've spent hours in the presence of dogs now, and I'm more comfortable with them. I believe if you gave me a chance, you'd be surprised at what I can do."

Chris regarded me with that flat look in his eyes. I held my breath, hoping that he might see the truth in my words and at least accept the interview. Then he shook his head.

"Martin, you're a good worker. You really care about your work, instead of going through the motions. I've put a lot of thought into your desire to have a higher position, and I've come to the conclusion that, right now, you don't have the qualities I need."

It felt like I'd been punched in the stomach. It was all I could do to keep from doubling over. Disappointment spread through my veins like poison.

"I can see you're upset," Chris commented. "And since we're having this conversation, let me tell you what I think you should work on. Your inability to work with dogs is first and foremost.

"Secondly, you just don't have any managerial qualities right now. You don't have the in-charge, go-getter attitude I would look for. I can't envision you telling someone to do something, or following up on an action that didn't go accordingly."

He was calling me weak. He was saying that I wasn't manager material. He could use all the polite words and proper phrases he wanted; it all came down to the same thing.

And he was right about all of it, except that part about not being a go-getter. I knew everything that needed to be done; I just liked to know what the person above me would prefer I do first. I knew what I would do, but I wasn't in a position where I could make those kinds of decisions.

Explaining that to him, that I was acting as my position demanded, would only work against me. He'd say something about my lack of ambition.

Maybe I wasn't ambitious, but I knew what I wanted. If I couldn't achieve my goal here, I'd have to do it somewhere else. Maybe I could open my own pet store someday.

"Martin?"

I lifted my head. "Thank you for hearing me out," I said.

Chris nodded. "Anytime. If, at some point in the future, you feel that you're better equipped for a higher position, come talk with me again."

"I will." Except I knew I wouldn't. I had made that decision already. By the time I was better equipped, I wanted to be my own boss.

"In the meantime, I'd like for you to work with the fish tanks. Clean them, make sure they're all working as they should be. Check the charts for the specifications."

I nodded and walked away, rubbing my stomach as annoyance made me fizzle inside. I practically had those charts memorized. I wasn't some newbie who couldn't tell the difference between saltwater and freshwater fish.

"Psst!"

I jumped and turned to see Quincy crouched near the ferret cage. He brandished a rag in one hand and a spray bottle in the other. The stench of vinegar-based cleaning solution surrounded him like a cloud.

"Hey," I said. "I didn't expect to see you here."

Quincy grimaced. "Bad luck at the interview."

At least I wasn't alone in my job troubles. Quincy switched subjects. "I'd trade you fish for ferrets any day."

Ferrets were carnivores. Their food was extremely high in protein, which led to some pretty rich-smelling cages, especially when said cage had been left to sit and ferment for weeks.

I was about to make a joke about shitty work when I realized what his comment actually meant. "You overheard me talking to Chris?"

Quincy winked. "Couldn't help it when I was right there."

I smiled a little. "Well, now you know that all my thinking didn't pay off. I'm back at square one."

"Hey, you tried. That counts for something."

"I kind of fudged the truth a little bit," I admitted. "About the whole dog thing. My boyfriend is a firefighter. With two Dalmatians. I've been near them, but I haven't actually interacted with them much. I guess Chris knew I was lying."

Being able to call Lance my boyfriend was the only upside to this situation.

Quincy frowned. "Your boyfriend's a firefighter?"

"Yes."

"I didn't know that. You should be careful."

That was baffling. "Why?"

He shrugged his shoulders. "I'm just saying. That's kind of a risky profession. Especially with this crazy fire stuff that's been happening lately. Anything could happen to him."

Disturbed, I cut the conversation short and went to tend to the fish tanks. Power had been turned off during the past couple weeks, and many of the tanks were filled with algae and dead fish that we hadn't been able to save.

The smell was strong, like a swamp. Pretty much the only tanks in good shape belonged to the bottom feeders and the snails, who were self-cleaning.

I headed into the back and pulled on a pair of gloves so I could get to work.

Honestly, I was a little relieved that I'd been rejected by Chris. I had a definite answer. There was no more guesswork involved. I could move on from here.

This place wasn't right for me, not now. I wasn't the same guy I used to be. I had a boyfriend now.

I knew I was worth something, even if it wasn't all that much yet. I'd overcome some of my fears. Maybe … no, definitely, I would keep growing. I'd become more capable.

If I could get over this weird stomach thing, I'd almost feel amazing.

For now, I had fish tanks to clean and algae to scrape. So that was what I did.

Chapter 19 - Lance

I shredded the letter into tiny strips, then tore those strips into smaller bits. Soon enough, all that remained of my correspondence with that lawyer bastard was a pile of confetti.

The letter had begun with an apology instead of a greeting, which had told me all I needed to know. I read it anyway, feeling each word jab at me like quick strikes of an ice pick into my heart.

There was nothing that could be done to help me with the dogs. They would not ever belong to me unless Chief Patrick handed them over.

The end.

Growling to myself, I swept the scraps of paper to the side and put my head in my hands. There had to be something else I could do. There was always another option, wasn't there?

I could buy a puppy.

With Martin at my side, we could pick a pup out of a litter and raise him as our own. Then that dog would be mine, and no one could take it away from me.

That was fine if all I wanted was a pet, but I didn't want any old companion. I wanted my Spot and Dottie, my best friends.

Could I blackmail Patrick, doing the same to him as he'd done to me? Unfortunately, I had nothing to back up any threats I made. Patrick almost certainly had fabricated evidence that he could use against me. So that was out of the question.

Option two was … give up.

I growled again, and it turned into a moan. I flopped my arms across the table and set my head down between them.

"You don't look like you're doing anything useful."

Opening my eyes, I saw Shep approach. I grimaced at him. "I don't need you on my case right now, Shepherd."

Shep flopped down into the chair on the other side of the table. He kicked his legs up, putting his boots by my face.

Disgusted, I sat up and swatted his legs off the table. "Don't you have manners?"

"It got you to stop moping, didn't it?" he teased. His eyes glittered with amusement, as always. "You were being such a waste of space, I figured I'd come join you."

"This station isn't big enough for the two of us wastes of space," I grunted. "I'd fight you for the honor, but I really don't care enough right now."

"It's kind of sad that the only way I can win is if you forfeit." Shepherd rubbed his chin, his fingers rasping over stubble. "You're so good at everything, even slacking off."

"I wish," I sighed.

"What's wrong, Lance?" He tilted his head, looking at me as if he actually cared.

Might as well tell him, since he's the only real friend I've got here.

"I'm still having trouble with the dogs. There's nothing I can do. Except I'm starting to think that might be for the best."

I rubbed my temples, confusion rising inside me. "I haven't been able to spend as much time with them as I'd like.

I just got into a relationship. Maybe it'd be best if I gave them over to someone with more time to give to them."

Shep whistled out through his teeth, a high-pitched, warbling sound. "Oh, you know, that's how it usually is. It's either the pet or the boyfriend. You can't have both if they clash."

I'd heard that mindset before, and it usually led to jokes about needing someone to come take ownership of the boyfriend. I hadn't considered it in this context, and it brought a heavy question to mind.

If it came down to it, would I choose Spot and Dottie, or Martin? Who demanded more of my priorities: the ones who had been with me all along, or the man I was just now beginning to understand?

"It doesn't have to be like that," I grunted. I slapped my palm on the table and stood up. "I won't let us be like that."

Shepherd gazed up at me, unusually serious. "I don't want you to get hurt," he said. "So you'd better prepare for disappointment."

I didn't answer. Even though I knew he was speaking logically, giving good advice, I didn't want to do as he said. There had to be some way to handle all of this, if only I searched hard enough.

Something told me time was running short. I'd best not waste any.

Chapter 20 - Lance

I wasn't any closer to coming up with a miraculous solution by the time I went home for the day. Not that I had much time to think when there was work to be done.

As always, I felt a ton lighter than I had all day once I walked through my own front door. Spot and Dottie flanked me like guardians, tails wagging low and slow.

Martin wasn't anywhere in sight.

A knot of worry formed in the back of my throat. "Martin?" I called. No answer. I hadn't expected one. Nothing could ever be easy.

The dogs didn't seem to be too worried, though. They didn't sense danger. Swallowing hard, I followed their lead and tried to act normal. I did what I did every single day, and took them back to my bedroom.

Halfway down the hall, I started to hear a distinctive rushing sound. The shower. My spirits rose, and I laughed at myself for being so stupid, going off and jumping to conclusions like that.

I stuck the dogs in my room and fed them, then let them be.

I headed to the bathroom, finding the door standing ajar. Steam billowed through the gap, perfumed with the scent of soap. I crept through the doorway and undressed, letting my clothes fall silently to the floor. Pulling back the curtain, I stepped into the tub.

Martin was waiting for me, wrapping his arms around me. I pressed my lips to his, growling softly with appreciation at how good he felt against me. He was slick with soap and very warm, a living fire.

Nuzzling my nose on his, I detected something a little off and leaned back. "You smell like fish."

He laughed. "Why do you think I'm in here? You could help, you know."

I was only too happy to assist, grabbing the bar of soap and working up a lather in my hands. Rather than use the bar itself, I rubbed my hands over Martin's body. I relished in the feel of his soft, slick skin underneath my fingers. I stroked his back, down to his ass, paying special attention to each cheek.

Martin arched his back and pressed his ass against my hand. I pushed my body closer to his and breathed hotly against his ear. He tilted his head, offering his ear to me. I nibbled at his ear lobe, tugged on it.

"You make it hard to focus on getting clean," I growled to him.

In answer, he rubbed himself against me. I slid my finger between his ass cheeks and teased his opening, making him gasp. With my hand slick with soap, my touch glided over him as if I was using lube. I didn't push inside him, though. I pulled my hand away and kept rubbing soap over his body, up to his shoulders and neck.

His muscles were tense.

Concern opened up inside me. I started to massage his shoulders, working his stiff muscles. "You had a tough day?"

Martin leaned against me and sighed, tilting his head forward to give me better access to his neck. "I finally asked my manager about moving up to a higher position at the store. He turned me down."

My heart twisted. I kept one hand on his neck and wrapped my free arm around his waist, hugging him to me. "I'm sorry, baby."

I'd never called him baby before. The word just came out, so naturally I hardly noticed.

Martin jumped with surprise against me, and then he seemed to reach the same conclusion I had. "It's okay. I pretty much knew that was going to happen."

"Still. That has to suck. But at least you haven't completely lost your job, right? You're still good with that?"

"Yeah," he sighed. "Not that I can be sure of how good that is. It seems like a dead end. Maybe I should … oh!"

Martin jumped as I worked my soapy hand around to his front, rubbing his stomach and thighs. My wrist brushed against his groin.

"Keep going," I breathed. "I'm listening."

He trembled against me, but pulled in a deep breath and continued. "I had an interesting conversation with a coworker. He told me I should be careful about being in a relationship with you."

I grunted, somewhat surprised, but not really. "I had a similar conversation with another firefighter. I think I've decided not to listen to him."

"Me too," Martin said. "They don't know what they're talking about."

I smiled and kissed his cheek, enjoying the way he hunched his shoulders up at the rasp of my stubble on his skin. "I'm glad we're in agreement. Now I think I have just the thing for you. For stress relief."

Martin giggled and turned in my arms to face me, tilting his head back to look up into my eyes. "Just for stress relief. Don't go expecting anything else."

I let my hand wander down slightly, my fingers brushing over his dick. He bucked his hips, rubbing himself against me. I kissed him and growled against his lips, holding onto him and teasing him with light, quick little tugs. He grabbed at my back and dug his nails into my skin.

Desire had my cock stiff, erect to its full length. I was pushed hard against his thigh, rubbing on him, stoking my lust for him.

Giving in to the urge, I tightened my fingers more around him, stroking him longer and slower until he was gasping and trembling. His forehead pushed against my shoulder and he whispered breathlessly to me, urging me on, demanding that I bring him all the way.

Sliding my hand all the way to the base of his shaft, I pulled my hand up to his tip and worked it with my thumb.

That was all it took to drive him over the edge. I felt a rush of heat against my hand and leaned back to watch his face while he finished. His mouth was open, his eyes closed. He looked like he was in heaven.

After a few minutes, he opened his eyes and blinked at me. I felt him grab me and moved eagerly against him, wanting to have my turn.

Shep and Martin's coworker had been looking out for us, sure. They'd been saying what they thought was best. Nice of them, but I wasn't going to let their opinions mess with us. We had our own thing going, and it was going to continue despite all the doubts and worries.

I stopped thinking as Martin started to work on me, focusing on him, the shower, and the way we felt together. The rest of the world didn't exist right now, and that was how I wanted it to be.

Chapter 21 - Lance

Everything went pretty well for about a week after that. There still weren't any answers for anything. However, we had each other, and that was all that mattered.

Then, as I was working at the site of the fire, hosing down flames, something happened to disturb the peace.

"Hey, Lance."

I turned my head, making sure to hold the rest of my body in the same position so I wouldn't mess with what I was doing with the hose. Shepherd strode up to me, lifting his hand as he saw me looking at him.

I started to greet him, then frowned. We were down to working on the fire with a single team at a time, and he wasn't on this one.

I saw his truck down the road and frowned deeper. He'd come out this way under his own power. Why?

"What are you doing here?" I asked, shouting over the sound of the pounding rush of hose water.

"Need to talk to you," he hollered.

I nodded down at the hose I held in both hands, signaling to him that I was kind of busy. Shep sighed and shuffled his feet. He looked pretty nervous, which wasn't an expression I was familiar with when it came to him.

That got my hackles up. What the hell was so wrong in the world that it made *Shepherd* look unnerved? The guy was unflappable, mostly because I didn't think he recognized stress when it stared him in the face.

Shepherd moved away and I lost track of him for a little bit, working on the fire. A minute later, he returned, dragging someone else from my team with him. A replacement. He was pretty serious.

I was curious now, so I transferred my hold on the hose over to my replacement. Once I was sure that they were in the right position, I moved away and followed Shep a good distance away, so we wouldn't have to scream at each other to have a conversation.

"What is it?" I asked. "Kind of busy out here, Shep."

Shep nodded. He swallowed, his Adam's apple bobbing up and down. More signs of nervousness. "I'm here to bring you back to the station. The chief wants to talk to you in private."

No. Dammit, no. Why can't he leave me alone?

My heartbeat picked up. I fought hard to keep my nervousness from showing on my face. "What does he want?"

This could be for something completely innocent. I had a couple of things that Chief Patrick definitely might like to talk to me about — the dogs, the fires — but this didn't have to be one of those.

This could be unrelated. I shouldn't get all riled up based on a few sentences of information. At the same time, I knew deep in the back of my mind that this was not going to be easy. It never was.

Shepherd shrugged. "I don't know. He grabbed me from traffic duty and sent me to come find you."

A couple of stop lights were out of commission downtown, due to construction work. In a quieter area, the burned-out light would turn into a self-regulated four-way stop.

Since downtown was typically a lot busier and drivers were more impatient, a cop or a firefighter went out and acted as a crossing guard, directing the traffic. It was grueling, boring work, especially in this heat.

Kind of explains why he looks so disheveled. Could be reading the signs wrong. He's not nervous. Just tired.

Well, there was nothing I could do about it. The chief wanted to see me, so I was going to go see him.

"You going to give me a ride to the station?" I asked.

Shep nodded and jangled his keys at me.

We had the air conditioning on full blast during the ride back to the station. My sweat dried on my arms and forehead, cooling me a little. Worst thing about working with fires for a living wasn't really the smoke or the danger, as far as I was concerned. It was the sensation of being cooked alive in your suit by waves of heat, like a baked potato wrapped in foil, roasting in the oven.

Dropping me off, Shep bid me good luck and drove away, presumably to return to his work as a human stoplight.

Looked like if I was to go back to the fire, I'd be taking my own truck.

But first, I had to get through this talk with the chief.

I went to his office, mentally preparing myself the whole way. His office door was open and he sat inside at his desk, fiddling with one of his many stacks of paper. However, he didn't seem to actually be doing anything. I watched him for a minute, as if I could figure out what he wanted from me by observing him.

"Are you going to stand there all day?"

I jumped, startled. Embarrassment flooded through me at the realization he'd known I was watching him all along. I stepped inside and shut the door behind me.

I didn't sit. Not yet. Sitting would mean committing myself to this, and I wasn't willing to do that yet.

Chief Patrick pushed his papers aside and studied me with an intense look on his broad face. "I'm going to cut to the chase here, Lance. We need to keep the trend going."

It isn't about the dogs.

I said nothing, biting my tongue.

"We can't have another fuck-up like this one. You know that, don't you?"

It hadn't been my fault. I'd started this fire in the same manner as I'd started all the others. Something must have happened, an errant gust of wind, or there was even the possibility some delinquent had come along and decided to add fuel to the literal fire. There was no way of telling.

This particular blaze had been going on for so long that any examinations would really only be able to pinpoint the starting location. All other evidence would be burned away to nothing.

"You'll have to be very careful. It will need to be extremely small, in a public area. What about Brighton Park?"

"No!"

The denial jumped to my lips before I could stop myself from saying anything. I'd promised Martin I would never start another fire. I'd be damned if I was going to break that promise by starting one at his favorite fucking park.

Patrick's gaze was flat and threatening. "What do you mean, no? You haven't forgotten our deal, have you? What's at risk?"

I bit my tongue, focusing on the bright spot of pain, using it to hold myself together. "Why so soon? The last fire isn't even out yet. We've only just contained it."

"You're lucky you have someone to tell you what to do," Patrick said. "You have no vision. No sense of imagination.

"Even fucked up, this last fire has been phenomenal for our image. We've gained so much attention. Our funding is secured. It might even be raised. There's no reason to let all of this fall aside. We have to keep going."

"But you just said it yourself. Our budget won't be cut now, at least not for the time being." I stared at Patrick, willing him to see the logic. "That was our goal. We accomplished it. The end."

"This is a fast-paced world. The moment we stop, all the attention will go to the next big thing. We must make sure that doesn't happen.

"You understand. Don't you? Or do I need to take an *extra step* to ensure that you do?"

I understood perfectly well. I shook my head, biting my tongue again. A dozen emotions fought inside me, each one as intense and shocking as the one before it. Fear, anger, trepidation, dread, and so many more.

"Good." Patrick nodded. "Think on it. Let me know the location you decide on so I can approve it."

"I'll think about it," I replied.

After that, he dismissed me, and I somehow made it back out to my truck. I sat there, shivering despite the heat.

I couldn't break my promise.

But if I didn't, the consequences would be far worse.

If I'd thought things were complex before, I hadn't been prepared for this. The question was no longer just where my priorities lay, but what I would do to be able to tend to those responsibilities.

At least I managed to keep from giving him a solid answer. He can't pin me to something if I can avoid it.

Unfortunately, he was a lot smarter than me. He'd figure out what I'd done, and I wouldn't be able to get away with it a second time.

Somehow, I got through the rest of the day and went home. As soon as I walked through the door, I smelled something cooking. Fragrant tomato sauce.

Must be pasta. For all Martin lacked in fancy cooking skills, he could make a damn good spaghetti dinner. Then again, everyone in the world could make spaghetti. It wasn't rocket science.

I tended to the dogs, as I always did, and went in search of my boyfriend. I found him in the kitchen, stirring a pot of bubbling sauce. In another pot, spaghetti noodles boiled.

The dining room table had been set, covered with a red tablecloth made of actual fabric, unlike the cheap, throw-away seasonal ones I tended to buy. Martin had obtained wine glasses from somewhere, and also a bottle of wine, all of which were also set up on the table.

My interest piqued, I came up behind him and wrapped my arms around him. I kissed his neck, amusement rising inside me as I realized he'd somehow gotten pasta sauce up here. I licked his skin and nuzzled my face against him. "What's the special occasion?"

Martin scrunched up his shoulders and wiggled around to face me. His eyes were bright, and a huge smile curved on his lips. "I figured I should enjoy something fancy before I'm not able to anymore. It's going to be a while before I'm able to drink alcohol again."

I tilted my head, trying to figure out what he was saying. "Not able to enjoy things anymore?" That sounded like an incredibly worrying thing to say, and yet he was beaming like it was the best news in the world.

Martin stood on the tips of his toes and kissed me. He whispered against my lips, "I'm pregnant."

Chapter 22 - Martin

Getting pregnant wasn't something I'd considered a possibility. I hadn't even thought about it. Despite my original plans being to have sex with Lance for the purpose of helping him to feel better, I hadn't thought about protection or anything like that.

Too late now. I was knocked up. I'd gone to the doctor after getting frustrated with being run down, and my bloodwork came back with an unexpected result. My mother's family had a history of blood-related problems, so the whole point of the blood test was to keep an eye on that to make sure we caught any developing issues inside me.

I expected that I might have a low white blood cell count or something. Something I'd been preparing for the possibility of my entire adult life.

But no. I was pregnant. I'd gone ahead and scheduled my first prenatal visit in another two weeks. All that remained had been for me to tell Lance.

I had no idea how he would take it, and I'd meant to be cautious, but excitement had gotten hold of me and before I knew it, I'd planned that special dinner.

Maybe it was going overboard. It was just a baby. People had them all the time.

But this was *my* baby. Even unexpected, I planned to raise it right. It wouldn't ever see the kinds of struggles I'd had with my own parents. Absolutely not.

It was going to be pampered and spoiled and loved, and I was going to make sure it had the confidence to go wherever it wanted in life. Everything my own parents had done wrong, I was going to do better.

The only downsides to this were Lance's potential upset, and my lack of a job capable of supporting an entire new human. I would make it work, though. I'd already fallen in love with the little life inside me, even though he or she had a habit of making me feel nauseous.

But, right now, as I looked up at Lance, I felt better than I had in a long time.

Lance stared at me, and I could see the gears turning in his mind as he struggled to process what I'd told him. His mouth fell open and his eyes went wide. They were blue with shock, like he had been frozen with surprise. "You … what?"

"I'm having your baby!" I said. Wrapping my arms around his shoulders, I pressed my stomach to his. "Can you feel it?"

Of course he couldn't, but he looked down between us with a puzzled, wondering expression. I laughed and kissed him. After a moment, he kissed me back.

"Are you sure?" he asked.

"Yes! I had a blood test at the doctor's office. And I'm going back in a couple of weeks for another appointment. Would you come with me?"

I waited, hopeful, nervous, as Lance looked at me, and a surge of emotions played across his face. He was afraid. Who wouldn't be?

He was stunned, and hesitant, and just generally didn't know what to make of the situation. He undoubtedly had some of the same questions I did, about how I was going to support this kid with my stupid grunt-level job.

He was also probably wondering what this would mean for himself and his own job. I had no idea if he wanted kids or a family. Spot and Dottie might be the only kids he had any desire to own.

Then Lance smiled. He tossed his arms around me and pulled my body more against his, engulfing me in his arms. He spun me around, laughing, and then set me back down on my feet.

"I can't believe this," he whispered, his voice wavering. "I never thought something like this would happen. I didn't think I would ever find someone."

"I'm not going anywhere," I said. That sounded a little too confident, so I amended it. "If you want me to stay, that is?"

"Do I want you to stay?" he echoed. "I want to have this kid with you. I want you to move out of that house of yours and in with me. Permanently.

"I want you to quit your job and marry me someday, be my house-husband. Have my babies."

All of that was far more than what I expected from him. I wanted all those things, too. I closed my eyes, letting relief flow through me and soothe my nerves.

So many of my concerns had just been put to rest. I could live with him. I could be with him while I figured out my … our future.

Opening my eyes, I looked up at him and nuzzled my nose on his. "You just want me where you can keep an eye on me," I teased.

"Damn right." He kissed me, and I melted into his arms.

We ate dinner and then spent the rest of the night talking, making tenuous plans for the future. I couldn't move in with him permanently until I officially moved out of my old house, which was currently out of reach in a dangerous place. So that would have to wait.

And I wouldn't quit my job just yet. I had plenty of months of work left in me. And after that, well, I would be spending a lot of time with the baby.

As for Lance, he shared with me that he had a sizable savings account. He wasn't much of a big spender, which I had figured out a long time ago. "Supporting the baby will be a piece of cake," he crowed excitedly. "I might even find a better job. A more stable job, so I can be home more."

However, it was at this point that he went suddenly quiet. We were sitting on the couch together. He had his back leaning against the arm and I was between his legs, leaning on him. I felt him grow still, and tilted my head back to look up at him, puzzled by the change in mood. "What is it?"

"The chief asked me to set another fire, baby."

Fear twisted in my gut like a knife. "You can't!"

"I'm not going to," he promised. "I thought about it, to keep him from blackmailing me, but there's no way I could do that to you. Not to our baby, either. I've always wanted a family someday, and I'm not going to fuck this up."

"Then what are you going to do?" The fire chief would never, ever let Lance leave, because he had a perfect thing going. If Lance so much as showed his desire to skip out, the chief would release all the blackmail, and that would be the end of our story.

Lance would be arrested. He'd be a convicted felon, put away behind bars. After all, he really had been the arsonist. There was no denying that.

"I'm going to go directly to the cops."

More fear stabbing me in the gut. I put my hand on my stomach and sat up, turning to face him. "That's going to be just as bad!"

"It won't," he promised. "You have to trust me on this. If I can get to them first and explain my side of things, I'll have a better chance. I can't let Patrick poison their minds with his lies."

"Do you really think that's going to work?"

Lance hugged me and pulled me tight to him. "It has to."

Chapter 23 - Martin

Though neither of us made the decision out loud, both Lance and I seemed to reach an agreement that we would wait until after my first prenatal visit to the doctor. We wanted to at least have that experience to carry us through what came next.

We held hands in the doctor's office, which was covered in charts and displays about the development of a fetus. Looking at the progress my unborn child would go through inspired a very real sense of wonder and anticipation inside me. Up until now, this had all felt kind of abstract.

But it was real. My baby was going to be the size of a grain of rice, then the size of a strawberry, then an apricot. He or she was going to develop hair and eyelashes and fingerprints. His or her heart would beat. He or she would test their limbs, explore their limits.

All of it in the comfort of my warm, loving stomach.

The visit turned out to be a lot of talking as the doctor went over what felt like a textbook's worth of information. The changes the baby would go through. The changes my body would endure, emotional and physical. Safe exercise, proper nutrition, appropriate sex practices. On and on and on.

Lance hung on every word, his expression that of a model student during a lecture. He was taking my pregnancy incredibly seriously. He was already refusing to let me do things for myself, opening doors, carrying things for me.

He looked so happy when he did that I didn't argue with him. And it was nice to be pampered.

Because of my family history of having blood-related problems, my visits to the doctor would be slightly more frequent. I would have a lot of scans and examinations and tests to endure, to ensure my baby was not at risk.

And there was an ultrasound, to make sure I looked good on the inside. My baby was invisible to me, just a tiny blob of multiplying cells, but I stared with wonder at the screen anyway. In eight months, all that empty space would be filled up with new life.

Lance's cheeks were wet as he pressed my hand to his lips. I cuddled closer to him, my heart swelling. With this next step taken, there was so much I needed to do.

First, we spent the day together. We caught a movie and fumbled around with each other in the dark, like horny teenagers. Two hours of foreplay awakened our appetites, and we took a picnic lunch out to Brighton park.

With the sun warming our backs and the smell of flowers on the wind, we ate and then fooled around on the blanket when no one was watching. After that, we went for coffee.

Lance looked at me across the table and said, "You told me you'd never been to the overlook with someone else. How about we change that?" My heart trembled in my stomach and I nodded, too breathless to speak.

Since it was a weekday, we had the river mostly to ourselves. Lance held my hand in his, and we walked together. I kept having to sneak looks at him, observing the reddish highlights in his hair, the eventual blush of sunburn on his cheeks and the back of his neck. He hardly seemed real.

I held his hand tighter, absurdly afraid he'd drift away from me if I let go.

Eventually, hunger drove us back into town for dinner. It really was the epitome of the perfect day. I had to marvel at how far I'd come. From the disappointing son of successful lawyers, to a man on the verge of starting his own family. How did something like this even happen?

It was all because of Lance.

Lance, who was the man he was in part because of the dogs he'd raised. They brought out the best in him.

I owed him, and them, the honor of properly meeting them before it was too late.

I looked over at Lance as we parked in the driveway. "I want to touch the dogs."

He looked at me in silence for a moment or two, taking in what I had said. The reason was written on my face, and he nodded slowly. "If you're sure."

"I'm sure."

I wasn't sure. I was terrified. But this was how it had to be. The time had come.

We went inside, and I stood in the middle of the living room while Lance fetched the dogs. They tried to politely ignore me, as per usual, but Lance walked them up right in front of me and told them to sit. Spot and Dottie sat, heads tilted and tails gently wagging with uncertainty.

This was the closest I'd been to a dog in years. It was both easier and worse than I had expected. They were there, and that was all. But, they were *there,* all big and close, with mouths full of fangs and huge paws studded with dull black nails.

If I made so much as a wrong move, I felt like I would be shredded to mincemeat in an instant. I held my breath, the urge to flee knocking around wildly inside me.

"Hold out your hand," Lance instructed.

This was it. The moment I had spent years avoiding. I stuck out my hand, my joints squeaking like rusty wheels. My palm was up, my fingers trembling.

Dottie was the first to lean forward, sniffing my hand. Her whiskers brushed my palm, tickly and gentle. Then she pushed her muzzle into my hand and licked my wrist.

The shock of her warm, wet tongue snapped something inside me. A wall I had erected years ago and worked to fortify ever since came crashing down.

A dog. I had touched a dog.

I dropped to my knees. Lance lurched as if to grab me. Ignoring him, I stared into Dottie's intelligent brown eyes, brought my hand to her neck, and petted her.

Soft, so soft. She nuzzled my hand, her head strong and broad and comforting to the touch.

A laugh bubbled out of me, and I raised my other hand to Spot. He skipped the whole sniffing part and shoved his head at me, demanding pets.

I flinched a little, and Lance once again made as if to interrupt. "I'm okay," I said. My voice shook, but I really was.

I felt light, like someone had thrown a switch inside me and turned off the gravity. The two dogs were so soft, so perfect, so gentle and eager. They wagged their tails so hard their entire bodies shook, their muscles trembling from holding back.

I kept petting them, touching them, as if I was trying to make up for all the years I had gone without. I was hardly aware of Lance until he crouched down beside me and wrapped an arm around my shoulders.

Spot and Dottie went crazy, overcome with pure animal joy that he had joined us. They swarmed over him, bouncing and pawing at him, mouthing his arms with gentle play-bites.

I backed off, their energy making me nervous again. Lance looked up at me and then back at the dogs. "Calm," he said.

Slowly, with a great effort, the dogs went still, though they trembled with excitement.

Standing us both up, Lance wrapped his arms around me. He kissed my lips, softly, gently. "Are you okay?" he asked. "I didn't know they were going to flip out like that."

I shook my head and hugged him tightly, letting my tremors calm fully. "I'm okay. Just … have to get used to it."

"I understand. But that was an enormous step you just took. I'm proud of you, Martin."

Maybe I couldn't fix everything going wrong right now, but I had mended this part. The second-most troublesome part of my life was over.

Why stop there?

Why not go ahead and deal with the most intense problem in my life right now?

Standing up, I grabbed my phone from my pocket. "I'll be back," I said. Lance watched me, his gaze knowing.

I headed for the bedroom for some privacy, feeling his eyes follow me all the way there. I focused on him and his support while dialing my mom's phone number. As the phone rang, I gathered my strength and resolve.

I was not a little boy who could be cowed by guilt tactics, not anymore. I had overcome a lot. I had accomplished so many things now. Even if those things weren't what my parents wanted, they were what *I* wanted.

All the prestigious job positions in the world would never equal my rediscovery of the love of dogs. Or the attention of the wonderful man who believed in me. Or the knowledge of the baby growing inside me.

Mom picked up on the fourth ring, as she always did. "Martin," she said, by way of greeting. She managed to sound hopeful and disappointed all at once, like I had already raised and lowered her expectations, despite not having said a word to her.

"Hey, Mom. You'd better get Dad and put me on speaker phone. I'm only going to say all of this once."

She didn't say anything. I waited, and still she said nothing. After a full minute went by, I decided I had spent enough of my time waiting, and started talking.

"I know both of you are still hoping I'll become a lawyer someday, after I've come to my senses. Well, I *have* come to my senses. I'm not going to come home. I'm not going to go to law school. I don't need to do that to be happy."

"Life isn't *about* being happy, Martin," Dad said, his voice heavy with disapproval.

"Maybe not *your* life. But I'm not you. I'm me. The friend I'm living with? He's my boyfriend. And I'm pregnant. I'm going to live my own life now."

My mother pulled in her breath with a hiss. At least that confirmed for me that I was on speaker phone. "Pregnant? How do you think you're going to be able to raise a child with your job? It's much too expensive for you."

"Lance and I will take care of the baby. We have it under control." And we did. I believed that.

Needless to say, my parents were not happy campers. I didn't care. I got through all of what I had meant to say, and ended with, "If you ever change your minds about me, I'd love to hear from you again. I love you. Bye."

And then I hung up before they could waste their breath saying anything else.

I did love them. I loved them as anyone loves their parents. For better or worse, I was who I was because of them. And, right now, I was the guy who was going to play with dogs until the sun came up.

Chapter 24 - Lance

I'd been in a lot of tough situations. I'd seen blood and gore and death at the scenes of car crashes. I'd seen abused, emaciated dogs shivering in dog houses in the middle of winter.

I'd faced down fires time and time again, and even caused some myself. I'd saved lives, and I had sat in the doctor's office with my pregnant boyfriend, surrounding by grossly fascinating pictures of alien-looking babies.

None of that came close to the experience of sitting in an interrogation room, surrounded by three cops whose faces I all knew. We were acquaintances, had drunk together, partied together at events. Sharon, Paulo, and Hank. I was under their scrutiny, examined by them like any other common criminal.

I'd come in here and said I had critical information to share about a dangerous suspect in the area. No one expected it to be me until I started talking. I had to watch their eyes glaze over with surprise, harden with suspicion. Friendly faces became dispassionate, calculating masks.

I spilled everything, prefacing all of it by explaining that I was kind of a pushover. I talked about the budget cuts, Chief Patrick's plan, the blackmail, the struggle for ownership of the dogs, which also served as another bit of incentive for me to do as the chief wanted.

I told them that he was hinting about another fire, and where he had suggested it could be.

I talked until my mouth was dry and I could talk no more.

Silence.

All three cops looked at me as if I had lost my damn mind, although I didn't know if they didn't believe me, or if they were astonished by the scale of corruption here.

Then, Sharon let out a hollow chuckle. She was a part-timer, a soccer-mom type if there ever was one: fifteen pounds overweight, platinum blonde hair, a little too much makeup. Right now, she looked like she'd just watched a beloved pet get snatched up by a hawk. "We kind of knew about all of this."

I started and stared at her. "What?"

She nodded, tucking her pen behind her ear. "We've been suspicious for a long time about all these fires. They couldn't be natural. We never found enough proof to do anything about it, though. And we never imagined it would be you, or that you would have such a terrible story to tell."

"I can't believe Patrick did something like this," Paulo snarled. Small and dark, he made a comical figure as he tossed his hands into the air with furious exasperation. "What a bastard, taking advantage of you like this."

The only one who hadn't said anything was Hank. He was the most experienced out of the whole group, and could usually be counted on to be a no-nonsense stickler for the law. I looked at him and asked, "Do you believe me?"

"I don't want to," he said. He pointed at his notebook. Everyone else had stopped taking notes about halfway through my story, but not him.

"But what you say sounds genuine to me. I have a hard time imagining you could make up such a detailed story if you hadn't gone through it all yourself. We'll have to have you repeat your story, and we'll have to verify it, to the extent that's possible. If we find any inaccuracies, that's the end of your believability."

"Are you going to arrest me?" I asked, very quietly. "If you do, I'm going to need someone to arrange to take care of the dogs. My boyfriend is pregnant. He can't do it on his own."

The three cops looked at one another. Hank stood up. "I think we need to discuss this in private, get a second opinion. Wait here, please."

I waited.

Before long, a second set of cops came in to talk to me. I repeated my story for them, sweating the entire time. I had to make them believe me. I had to be accurate, and sincere, in a way I never had before.

The worst part was, at the end of it, I couldn't tell whether or not they thought I was insane. They looked impassive, blank, like they wore masks.

Eventually, they also went away. The wait was longer this time. I spent every second staring at the floor and trying not to act guilty. I was almost certainly being watched through some hidden surveillance camera.

The door suddenly opened again, startling me. The person standing there was alone. Hank. He stepped inside and shut the door behind him.

In the few moments before he spoke, I realized I could smell my own nervous sweat. Was that a sign of guilt or innocence?

"After some deliberation, we have decided to believe you. In this case, we do not have any grounds on which to arrest you, since you were forced to do this against your will. This comes with a price, however."

"Anything," I said immediately. Not arrested? I didn't give a fuck what he wanted from me. If he wasn't going to arrest me, I'd do it.

"Think of this as a plea deal. In exchange for information, you'll be free to go." Hank folded his hands and leaned over the desk to look hard at me.

"We need every bit of information you've got. Every resource you used to start all the fires, and where you got them from. Your conversations with Fire Chief Patrick, in as much detail as you can remember. Everything.

"We'll be opening an investigation. It's going to be long and difficult. Dealing with important figures always is."

I nodded, relieved to have someone who knew what they were doing.

"Since it will be obvious that you're our informant, we are going to place you and your boyfriend in a safe house a few hours north. Patrick will not be able to find you or harm you in any way."

I had thought about this, and I kept nodding. Being far out of the way right now was a damn good idea. Patrick would know all this information came directly from me, and he would *not* be happy about it.

Hank stood up. "I'm going to fetch the sheriff so he can speak with you in private and make arrangements. But there is something else I want to tell you, about the Dalmatians you spoke of."

My heart sank. I gripped the edge of the desk. "What about them?"

"You were worried about what would happen to them. I spoke with our legal department; they have approved the decision to send the dogs with you into hiding."

I jumped out of my seat, knocking my chair over. "What?" I exclaimed, practically shouting. I was so fucking relieved I couldn't even think.

"So long as our investigation is underway, the two dogs could be at risk of harm if they stayed. They would potentially turn into bargaining tools.

"However, you will be disconnected from the fire department. That clears you to have custody of the dogs, for now. They can go with you.

"If we find out that the chief is truly guilty, there will be no contest about you maintaining full, permanent ownership. But don't get your hopes up. That is still far in the future."

I held my head, overwhelmed with joy flowing through my veins. I had been fighting this battle all along, and now the conclusion had been reached. Even though this wasn't what

I'd planned or hoped for, it was still a much better outcome than I ever could have imagined.

Spot and Dottie were going to be mine. The chief would be found guilty, while I remained a free, innocent man. Once the truth was revealed, I could go on and live a brand-new life with Martin and our baby.

Chapter 25 - Martin

The next few days were controlled chaos. I quit my job upon learning that I'd be expected to leave town with Lance, for potentially *months,* while the police hunted for evidence of Chief Patrick's crimes. No use sticking around when I was going to be taking so much time off I'd get fired anyway.

For what it was worth, Chris seemed genuinely sad to see me go. I wouldn't miss him, but I would miss everyone else, and the work, and the animals.

Lacking anything to do, especially while Lance was cooped up at the police station giving interview after interview and endless statements, I played with Spot and Dottie, discovering all their favorite places to be scratched and rubbed. Movements that came too suddenly still made me flinch, and I had to take breaks when it got to be too much.

However, they somehow seemed to realize that, and switched to playing with each other when they wanted to get rough. They were even smart enough to let me win at their games, when they could easily play tug with each other for hours before collapsing from exhaustion.

Eventually, the time came when we were rescued from our limbo. Lance came home one night, guided by a police cruiser. He came to me and wrapped his arms around me, holding me very close.

I nestled in against him, laying my head on his chest to listen to his heartbeat. It was a little faster than usual. I would know, after all the times I'd cuddled up on him like this. "Are we leaving?" I whispered.

He nodded against the top of my head, his chin rubbing on me. "First thing tomorrow morning. We need to pack. Can't take too much. We're trying to be discreet. I can take you back to your place real quick if you want to grab something."

I thought of all I had left behind, and somehow found myself shaking my head. "You're all I need."

"No clothes?" he teased. I heard his heartbeat slow down a little, and nuzzled my cheek on his, then nibbled his lower lip.

"Who needs clothes? We're going to be in hiding, sitting in a safe house all day. No need to get dressed if we're not going outside."

Lance made a growling sort of purr against the top of my head. "You have a good point. I guess not having clothes will free up a lot of extra space for dog toys."

I laughed and tilted my head up to kiss him. I melted against him and closed my eyes to soak in the feel of him, luxuriating in the heat of his body. I hadn't been kidding about going around naked. If we had a lot of time to kill, we might as well spend it in a fun way.

We spent the rest of that night packing our bags. One for us, and another, much larger, for Spot and Dottie. The dogs followed us around with their ears perked up, clearly curious about what was going on.

"I've never even gone on vacation with them," Lance commented while counting socks. "They have no idea what we're doing."

"They'll figure it out pretty fast when we're spending several hours in a car. Do we know where we're going?"

"No." Lance shook his head. "I guess we'll know when we get there, won't we?"

Part of me was worried about how out-of-control this situation was. We had no say in anything now. We didn't know where we were going, or how long we would be there, or even if the investigation would succeed.

By going to the police, Lance had ensured that we became a part of something much larger than ourselves. Patrick was, by all reports, very crafty. I wouldn't be surprised if he pulled some sort of trick.

But there wasn't anything I could do about it. I had to try to take care of myself and the baby as best as I could.

That night, all four of us slept in the same bed. Lance curled himself around me, and the dogs lay at our feet.

Very early the next morning, before dawn had even broken across the sky, Lance's phone rang. Rubbing my eyes, I sat up beside him and listened in to his half of the conversation. Not that there was much to hear, since he was mostly agreeing with whoever was on the line.

When he hung up, he reached over and wrapped his arms around me. He let his head rest on my shoulder.

I slid my fingers into his hair and hugged him tight. "Is it time?"

"Yeah. They want us to drive separately to the edge of town. Me first, then you five minutes later. We'll be getting into a car together there, and our own vehicles will be taken and hidden. No one will know where we've gone."

I nodded and kissed his cheek, then his lips. Wrapping my hand around his chin, I looked into his turquoise eyes. "Let's get going, then."

We packed our bags into our respective vehicles. Then we gave each other a final kiss, taking our time with it, letting our lips linger together.

Lance guided the dogs into his truck and buckled them in. Then he was gone, leaving a cloud of dust in his wake.

My heart throbbed to see him go, even though I knew I'd be joining him in five minutes. I didn't want to be separated from him for even a second.

As soon as I could, I followed after him. I reached the designated spot: a narrow side road leading through a field which was currently not seeing any use. A police cruiser and an unmarked car were already there waiting, while Lance's truck was nowhere to be seen.

I soon found out why when I stepped out with my bag. Two police officers emerged from the cruiser, while another person emerged from the other car.

One of the cops gestured to the unknown driver, who wore all black and a pair of sunglasses. "Martin, this is Scott. Scott is an agent who specializes in assisting with witness protections in northern California. He will be taking you to the safe house and will remain nearby. If you need anything, he'll be the one to get it for you."

That's a lot of information all at once.

"It's nice to meet you," I said.

Scott gave a brisk nod. So he wasn't a very talkative man.

The other cop held out his hand. "I'll be needing your car keys. Do you have anything else you need to get first, before you leave?"

I shook my head. There was finality in my denial. I couldn't turn back even if I wanted to, so I handed over my car keys and followed Scott over to the unmarked car. He took my bag and put it in the trunk, then opened one of the back doors for me to get inside.

Lance was sitting up front. I hadn't been able to see him because of the dark tinted windows. With me in the back were Spot and Dottie, their white fur already covering the interior.

"Hey, baby," I said, leaning over and kissing his cheek. He turned his head and met my lips with his, his eyes dark and narrowed. The kiss was fierce, needy, and I put my all into it to let him know I was okay.

"I'm glad you made it," he growled. "I was worried that something might happen. Patrick..."

He was going to worry like that anytime I went out of his sight for more than a second from now on. We were essentially fugitives, biding our time until we could come out of hiding. Me being pregnant probably didn't help the overwhelming protective feelings coursing through his veins.

I wasn't worried, though. With the police department and Lance on my side, there was no way anything bad could happen.

The driver's side door opened and Scott slipped inside. Without looking back at me, he said, "Buckle your seatbelt, please."

"Only because you said please." I grabbed the belt and pulled it over my stomach. I thought I had to use a bit more belt than I had in the past, although that might have been my imagination. Or, hell, maybe I'd gained some weight. I couldn't cook worth a shit, but Lance could.

Scott kept his face forward and seemed to be waiting for something. I peered out the windshield and saw one of the cops give him a signal. At that, he started driving.

There was silence in the vehicle for a good ten minutes. I cuddled up with the dogs and listened to the sound of the tires crunching over the loose gravel of this terrible road. This really wasn't an area meant for regular vehicles, although big, sturdy farm equipment would have no problem navigating the rough terrain.

Soon enough, we joined with the highway, and the ride became much smoother. I watched as Scott set the cruise control, his posture relaxing in such a minuscule way that I wouldn't have noticed it had I not been looking at him.

"Sorry for the brusque treatment," he said. He glanced over at Lance, then peered at me in the rearview mirror. "I wanted to focus on getting us safely out of the area. We didn't know if Patrick might have had someone watching."

"That's fine," Lance said, his voice grudging. "Makes sense."

"Martin?"

"Sure," I said. "I get it."

"Good." Scott nodded. He paused for a moment while passing another vehicle. "I'm sure both of you are aware of the arrangement being made, but it's part of my job to make sure we're all on the same page.

"I am taking you to a safe house north of here, near a very small town called Hornbrook. We will be leaving the interstate soon, and following a longer route, to make sure we're not followed.

"Once we reach the safe house, you will be required to remain inside at all times unless you give me plenty of warning in advance. I am your contact with the police, so all communication will be through me."

All of that made sense so far, but I did have a pretty pressing question. "What about my baby? I'm pregnant. I just had my first appointment."

"How soon did you need another?" Scott asked immediately. Nothing fazed him. Of course, he'd probably already known I was pregnant.

"I'm kind of at risk for some blood-related complications. My baby, too." I placed my hand on my stomach protectively. As if agreeing with me, Dottie rested her cheek against my abdomen.

"Once we have you all settled in, I will make arrangements with a clinic for your appointments. We'll follow a strict procedure to get you there and back without anyone seeing you, but it will be done. Don't worry about that."

Scott glanced at me again, and I saw a comforting smile on his face. "In fact, don't worry about anything. My job is to get you anything and everything you need.

"The two of you should just relax, and consider this an unexpected vacation. It's quite beautiful up north. I might be able to take you to the mountains for some trips, if that's something you're interested in."

Listening to Scott, I did relax. He was right. This was his job. All Lance and I had to do was bide our time.

The drive lasted nearly four hours, with a pit stop halfway through for lunch and to let the dogs stretch their legs. It was scenic much of the way, with the road winding and twisting through areas of vast forest. Low mountains edged the sky in the distance, coming closer the further we went.

Near the end of our journey, Scott turned off the main road. We passed through a lot of campgrounds, which were quite nice at first, but which started to devolve into piles of trash the deeper we went. We went so far that the roads turned to dirt trails covered with detritus. Several times, Scott had to get out to clear our way.

Then there weren't any campgrounds at all for a very long way.

"This area we're in now is protected property," Scott said. "Surrounded by surveillance cameras. Publicly, it's a nature preserve. Privately, it's a safe location, away from prying eyes. We've had a lot of estranged politicians, important figures, and illegal refugees out here before."

"That last one kind of doesn't fit," I said.

Scott shrugged. "If you want information from someone about the state of the country they've just left, you shelter them. We get information, and they eventually get fabricated documents and a new life here. A fair trade. Here we are."

At first, I didn't see anything. The trees were too thick. Then he drove a little further, and the trees parted to reveal a pretty little red cabin with a covered porch and a chimney. Where everything else looked a little wild and was even falling down in some areas, the cabin was in perfect shape.

Scott helped us bring our bags inside and gestured around the interior. "This is it. Everything runs off an underground generator, so you're officially off the grid. I'll be here every day or so to check out the genny and refuel it if necessary. You've got a bathroom and a kitchen fully stocked with essentials. There's a TV, but it has no signal. Plenty of movies, though.

"I'll be staying nearby. I'll be here in ten minutes if you need anything."

After that, there really wasn't much to do or say. This was where we would live, and honestly, I wasn't all that upset about it. Coming out all this way, I never would have expected to have access to all these modern amenities when we were basically in the middle of nowhere. It was borderline miraculous.

Once he made sure we knew where everything was, Scott left to go wherever it was that he was staying.

Then we were alone.

Footsteps behind me, and a warm presence as Lance wrapped his arms around me. He settled his chin on my shoulder, hugging me tightly. "I know this isn't where we thought we would be right now. But at least we're together."

I turned in his grasp and wrapped my arms around his neck. "I couldn't ask for anything better," I whispered. I nuzzled my lips on his, rubbing them together as I spoke. "We're safe. The baby's safe. That's all that matters to me."

"I think you're right about us being safe." Lance sighed. "I don't see how Patrick could have followed us, or had someone follow us. It feels weird to relax, though."

"Maybe I could help with that?" I suggested.

Lance smiled for me as I slid my hand down between us, settling on his crotch. "What do you say we get started on the whole naked thing and break our new bed in?"

I was only too happy to lead him away by his rapidly-hardening member. We probably should have talked some more, since there were definitely things we had to say to each other. I wanted to tell him that everything would be okay from now on. That I loved him. But we had plenty of time for that. What I couldn't say, I could show him with actions.

Chapter 26 - Martin

Pretty quickly, Lance and I settled into a new routine.
We were cleared by Scott to spend time outside in the
surrounding forest, so long as we stayed within sight of our
cabin. He also made us carry a portable radio, which he
delivered before we went out on our first walk. The radio
would serve as our means of emergency communication with
him, since our cell phones were basically just fancy clocks this
far from civilization.

The precautions taken didn't let us forget why we were
out here in the first place. Patrick was never far from our
thoughts, especially for Lance.

Sometimes I woke up to find him pacing and pacing,
staring out the windows as if watching, waiting. It was like he
expected something to go wrong, though he pretended
otherwise with me.

We ate breakfast in the morning and then spent time
with the dogs. Being around them grew easier, slowly but

surely, though there were still times when one of them would take me by surprise and I would forget how to breathe.

Around noon, we often went outside for a walk around the perimeter, straying a little farther each day. As much as it stayed the same, the forest held new surprises for us each day.

New flowers and patches of mushrooms sprouted. We collected feathers, examined paw prints, and saw plenty of birds. If we stayed out on the porch at dusk, deer and raccoons wandered right past us without a care in the world.

We even saw a bear once, although it turned out not to be a bear, but a big black stump in the distance. Pretty scary, either way. At night, we had coffee and dessert, watched movies, fucked, and talked about the future.

We saw Scott every day, sometimes only for a moment or two as he checked out our generator. He brought us supplies every week, and occasionally stole me away to a hospital to have my tests performed and my ultrasounds done. Those excursions were unnerving, because of the secrecy with which they were carried out.

The threat of Chief Patrick lingered around every corner. Even though he was still in Red Bluff, I couldn't help but feel that way.

The good news was, the baby was growing right on schedule. Pretty soon, I was able to hear its heartbeat for myself, and that brought a new influx of intense emotion.

Somehow, months passed. Little problems came and went. Spot got the sniffles, and so did Dottie.

Lance fell in a bush, and I spent the rest of the night removing all the ticks that had taken advantage of his abrupt entrance into their territory. It was kind of hilarious, the way he thrashed around and whined like he was being murdered. Such a big alpha, you'd think he'd have some pain tolerance.

I got fat and developed some of the warning signs of anemia, dizziness and shortness of breath, on top of all the other normal pregnancy complications. I went on medication to combat the condition, which would hopefully regress after my pregnancy. The baby showed no signs of any illness, for which I was extremely thankful.

Updates from Red Bluff were slow, few and far between. It had never occurred to me just how much of a police investigation was procedure and paperwork. For every path they wanted to pursue, the cops needed to write about it, get it approved, and enact it.

Sometimes, the process wasn't that smooth, and they were rejected. The deeper they dug into Chief Patrick's life, the more complicated things became.

Scott told us that Patrick had done basically everything he could to cover his tracks. Only after endless weeks of peeling back the layers of protection were they finally revealing his guilt. They'd unearthed suspicious purchases and "confession" letters, drafted in Lance's name, that had been hidden in the chief's filing cabinets alongside receipts and inspection forms.

Some of the things he said didn't add up, either. He kept slightly changing his explanations.

Things were looking up, really. Even Lance relaxed.

One day, as I entered my seventh month of pregnancy, Scott drove up and walked up to our porch, like he always did when bringing something to us. His expression was incredibly serious.

I was on the porch with the dogs, my hands on my stomach as the baby kicked. I felt slow, mentally and physically, and it took me a little while to realize that he had stopped right in front of me, and was apparently waiting for me to realize he was there.

"Oh, hi, Scott," I said. "What's up?"

"How are you today, Martin?"

I smiled. "I'm fine. Lance went inside to get a glass of water. If you put it on my stomach when the baby kicks, it wobbles all over the place. You want to see?"

Scott's lips quirked, a crack in his mask. "Maybe. I have something to tell you, first."

"Tell us what?" Lance asked, emerging from the cabin with a full glass in one hand.

"There was a breakthrough in the case," Scott said. "I just received word about half an hour ago that Patrick has been arrested."

I pushed up from my chair, staggering. Lance caught me. I pressed one hand against him to steady myself and stared at Scott.

"Really? He's really been arrested? We can go home?"

"That is not advisable," Scott said quickly. "The entire town is in shock right now. The police department is struggling, and the fire department is in disarray.

"If Chief Patrick has accomplices besides you, Lance, they have not yet been discovered. Returning now would put everything at risk."

"So we're supposed to stay out here until when?" I pressed. I didn't care very much for myself, but I could tell Lance was agitated. His body was stiff against mine.

"This case is being moved to a top-priority position. Arrangements are being made. The verdict should be reached in less than a month."

"Don't I need to go back to testify?" Lance asked. He held my hand tightly. I squeezed it, trying to comfort him.

"Since you left behind numerous statements, no. Your words are suitable to represent you."

As soon as Scott left, I tossed myself into Lance's arms. I kissed his face all over, my full, pregnant belly against his hard body. "Did you hear that?" I asked. "This is all going to be over soon."

Lance put his hands on my shoulders and looked at me. He'd been letting his beard grow out, making him look like an untamed mountain man. His eyes were wild to match, darker than the shadows beneath the trees. "Something tells me this isn't going to be easy. I have a bad feeling."

"I'm supposed to be the one having paranoia and mood swings," I teased him. I kissed the tip of his nose to get him to smile and rested my cheek on his. "We're over the hill. It's all downhill from here."

Things were about to go down, that was for sure. I just didn't know in what way. We should have been safe. We were protected, watched over. Nothing bad should have happened.

I should have trusted Lance's instincts, though, because the next day Scott returned to us. If I'd thought he looked serious before, he was now positively grave.

"Patrick has escaped custody," he said.

Chapter 27 - Lance

It was a major, avoidable fuck-up. Chief Patrick had been arrested and put in a jail cell after hours of grueling interviews. Whoever put him in the cell must not have been paying enough attention, because security cameras captured Patrick reaching out and swiping the key from his pocket through the bars as the cop turned away.

But he didn't leave right away. He bided his time, waiting until the middle of the night to lessen the chances of anyone seeing him sneak out. No one realized he was gone until the next morning, because apparently no one thought to check on him.

Idiots, all of them. Fucking idiots. He could be anywhere by now. He could be in a different fucking country.

Grabbing Martin, I shoved him behind me. He was in danger. The baby was in danger. I had to protect them at all costs.

"Get inside," I snapped over my shoulder. I spun to face Scott. "Does he know about this safe house?"

No answer. "Does he?" I demanded.

"Yes," Scott said, reluctantly. He looked disgusted. "Other counties have been assisting in the investigation. The deputy from another police department knew about it, having heard about it from the sheriff. They've used it in the past.

"He mentioned it within earshot of Patrick. We only found out about this afterward, when he conveniently remembered. He has been fired."

Being fired wasn't good enough. That stupid, stupid bastard had jeopardized everything.

Martin hadn't moved. "Get inside, dammit!" I snarled at him. *Think of the* baby *and go!*

"Lance," Martin said.

Scott cut him off. "There is a very good likelihood that he won't come here. It's too dangerous, and he almost certainly wouldn't take the risk. However, to be on the safe side, we're going to move you to a new location."

"Now?"

"As soon as I get approval. I'm expecting some correspondence, and I have to head back to my own place.

"Both of you need to stay inside, including the dogs. Don't open the door for anything. If you have an emergency need, use the radio. Understand?"

I glared at him and squared my shoulders. Yeah, I understood. Did he? Fucking idiot.

Scott gazed back at me. His gaze was cool in the face of my fiery anger, which felt like it was rapidly blazing out of control inside me. "I'll be back," was all he said, and he turned and piled into his car.

Smart man. If he'd said more than that, I probably would have kicked his ass.

Months and months of peace and smooth procedures, and there was a fuck-up at the last moment? How typical. These assholes had gotten careless. They'd put lives at stake. I would never...

Turning, I grabbed Martin in front of me and propelled him into the house. I shut and locked the door behind us and snapped off a command to the dogs. "Guard!"

Spot and Dottie went on immediate high alert, positioning themselves near the door.

Martin tugged on my hand, trying to get my attention. "Lance, calm down. It's going to be okay."

"No!" I snarled. He flinched, and my heart twisted. I mentally punched myself for directing my anger at him.

Out of all of us, he was the one who deserved to be hassled the least. What had he done? Gotten pregnant and tried to start a happy life? He was innocent, and I should protect him, not make him worry.

Reaching out, I pulled him into my arms and stroked his hair. "It's okay. You're right. I'm just worried about you and the baby.

"Go pack up our bags. As much as you can. We need to be ready for relocation as soon as Scott comes back."

Martin nodded and kissed me. His lips lingered on mine for a brief moment, and I relished their sweetness, savoring it. Then he waddled off, and I took up a position by the front door — but not before I took a detour to the armchair and removed a big, thick stick from behind it.

I had selected this stick because it had the approximate shape of a baseball bat, and it felt good in my hands. All the play sword-fighting I'd done with Martin during our exile had served the extra purpose of allowing me to find a suitable weapon.

He didn't know it was here. I hadn't wanted to worry him that I felt the need for a weapon. All the same, I was glad for it now.

Holding my makeshift bat, I waited for Scott to return. And waited. And waited some more.

Minutes passed. Five, ten. Martin returned with our bags, dragging them behind him one at a time. Still no sign of Scott.

You could normally hear him coming from miles away, because of the way the forest carried sounds. However, I didn't see or hear anything.

After another five minutes, I opened my mouth to tell Martin to go hide in the bathroom. It was easily the most defensible position in the house, and…

A jolt of cold fear slipped through my mind like a silver arrow, cleaving me in half.

The bathroom.

The fan in there didn't work worth shit, so we'd gotten into the habit of opening the window whenever we showered. Morning wasn't all that long ago, which meant the window was still open.

Which meant there had been a breach in our defenses. All this time, I had been paying attention to the wrong area.

Martin stiffened beside me, making a small sound that I felt more than heard. I turned and *he* was there, filling the doorway to the kitchen with his broad frame. His expression was amiable, though his eyes were like voids. Absent of emotion.

"Patrick," I hissed.

"Hello, Lance," Chief Patrick said. He lifted his hand from his side. He held a pistol, which looked almost comically small in his big hand. "I'm sorry I had to come all the way out here to bother you, but we have some unfinished business."

"I finished with you a long time ago," I said. I tightened my grip on my weapon.

Patrick saw my muscles flex. His gaze darted to my bat. In response, he pointed his gun at Martin, who stiffened and let out another of those soundless gasps.

"I'd advise you to toss that weapon aside. You might come to regret what happens if you take a swing at me."

I snarled, adding my voice to an ongoing chorus that I only now noticed. Spot and Dottie were on either side of me, growling. They had their lips curled, revealing sharp fangs.

Unfortunately, I hadn't taught either of them any attack commands. My job was to make things better, not worse. Even if they could attack in this situation, I was loathe to put either of them at risk.

And I couldn't put myself at risk, not if I wanted to be around to see my baby be born.

I tossed my stick to the side and lifted both my hands to show Patrick I was at his mercy. There wasn't much I could do about the way I looked; my shock and outrage written all over my face.

This can't be the end.

We had overcome so many challenges, pushing past difficult situations and intense conflicts. I had not come all this way only to fail the man I loved.

I had to keep him talking, give Scott time to show up. "Why are you doing this, Chief? You know it's over."

"I can't let my career end in ruin," he said. His voice was hoarse. "I've done so much for so many. It isn't fair.

"I can't do anything to stop it. I don't want to be around to see it. But before I take myself out, I'm going to take you with me. This is *your fault,* Lance, you fucking backstabber."

Chief Patrick lunged and grabbed Martin. I flinched and reached out, but the pistol swung in my direction.

Martin moved.

No, dammit! Don't protect me. I'm protecting you!

Patrick aimed the pistol back at Martin, pushing the muzzle against his head. The safety was off, his finger on the trigger.

"I'll kill him first. Then you. Then me. That way, you get to know what it's like to have your world fall apart around you."

I saw his finger tighten. Martin must have sensed the movement. He cried out. I leapt forward again.

And a black-and-white blur shot across the floor, flying through the air.

"Spot!" I yelled.

Patrick flinched and the gun fired, a bright flash and a concussive bark of sound. Spot hit Patrick, and the two fell to the ground, tangled together. The gun skittered away across the floor.

Leaping after it, I fumbled for it, missed, and then grabbed it and swung back around.

Patrick staggered to his feet, blood covering his chest. I wondered for a brief instant how he had been shot, when I hadn't pulled the trigger yet.

Then I saw Spot.

Everything in my body went limp all at once. I collapsed to my knees, my arms going limp at my sides. The gun clattered on the floor again, and I kicked it away, under the couch, where it couldn't be easily gotten.

Spot lay on the ground, small in comparison to the red puddle spreading around his body. His jaw worked weakly, and his paws twitched.

He was dying.

It was like watching my child die. Everything inside me that had gone loose suddenly tensed up all at once and I cried out, roaring out my grief and frustration and fury.

I didn't care about Patrick. Didn't care about myself. Didn't care about anything except my fucking *dog.*

Patrick ran right out the door, leaving a trail of bloody splotches. Staggering to my feet, I went over to Spot and crouched over him and put my hands over the gaping wound on his chest. Blood pumped up between my fingers, thick and red and sluggish.

Somewhere, Dottie was whining.

Impulses and information, reaching me but not registering. Spot was so warm and alive under my hands, struggling. God, how had this happened? How the fuck had this happened?

"Lance!"

I looked up at the sound of more footsteps. Scott pushed his way through the front door, holding his head. Blood covered half of his face, leaking from a nasty gash on his temple. Well, that pretty much told me why he hadn't come until now.

"Get an emergency vet on that fucking radio," I snarled at Scott. "Get the cops after Patrick — he was here! Get me the sheet from the bed, I need to put pressure on this wound."

Before Scott could move, I heard a weird splattering noise from behind me. Then, Martin's quiet voice. "I think my water broke. Ow."

The entire world was devolving into fucking chaos. There was so much going on now that I couldn't register it all. I felt almost calm, detached from everything.

I looked at Scott and said, "Ambulance might be a good idea, too."

Chapter 28 - Martin

Almost as soon as my water broke, the contractions started, and they felt worse than anything I'd experienced in my entire life. Spasms shook through my body, contorting me into shapes I never knew were possible. Each one was a wave of pain that washed away my consciousness, leaving me to flounder to the surface for another few minutes before being pulled under again.

Scott arranged for the emergency vehicles to meet us at the edge of the campground, which was as far as they could safely go. He helped Lance carry Spot to the car, wrapped in a sheet. I didn't even think the dog was alive anymore, he was so still.

Tears ran down my face, dripping from my chin. That poor baby didn't deserve this. As much as I hurt, my heart throbbing, I couldn't begin to imagine what this was like for Lance.

I couldn't reach out to him, though. The pain was so bad inside me, like something was cleaving me in half.

Dottie crouched on the floor in the back, letting out piteous whines that my own soul echoed. Things had been going so well, and now they were so fucked up. How could so much change over the course of a single day?

The chaotic drive through the woods at a too-fast speed didn't help my pain. I drifted in and out of awareness until we came to an abrupt halt, at which point a pair of EMTs crowded around my door and practically carried me over to the ambulance. In only a matter of minutes, I was being whisked away in another vehicle at break-neck speed.

There were a lot of questions being asked of me, and I answered them as best as I could, though my memory seemed to be shot and I couldn't hold onto a thought for more than a moment. My thoughts were like water, sliding fluidly out of my grasp.

Lance. Scott. Patrick.

Spot.

There were no windows in the back of the ambulance, so when we stopped and I emerged into the middle of a city, it was like culture shock. My brief forays out of the cabin hadn't really prepared me for the sense of displacement, like I no longer belonged in this world.

I was given a ride in a wheelchair to the delivery ward, and endured the same monotonous questions at the hands of at least three more people, all of whom seemed way too concerned over what was relatively minor anemia being controlled with medication.

Maybe they were given warning about what I'd just gone through. Might make my problems worse, cause complications.

The only complication I was aware of was a whole lot of pain.

I closed my eyes to suffer through another contraction. When I opened them, Lance was sitting beside me.

"Lance!" I cried out. "What are you doing here? Shouldn't you be with Spot?"

His dark eyes shimmered with emotion. He picked up my hand and held it tightly. "I can't be with Spot during surgery. I can be with you during labor."

"But..."

He stopped me with a kiss. His gaze was so intense I couldn't look away. "I want to be here," he whispered. "I love you."

"I love you," I murmured back, resting my head on his. Everything felt so out of control.

The chief was on the loose. Spot was hurt badly. Scott had been whacked pretty good, and was apparently getting stitches.

And I was giving birth a little early. One event after another, like a series of dominos crashing into each other.

Only Lance was unchanged. He was my rock right now, my source of strength. I took from him gladly and, as the pain grew worse and the contractions came closer together, I relied on him completely to keep my mind from snapping.

Even when it got to the point where my entire body felt like it was rejecting me, about to break in half, I felt his presence there with me.

And when he urged me to push, repeating the doctor's command, I pushed as hard as I could until I felt something slither out of me, followed by a relief so amazing it was euphoric. I saw stars behind my eyes and could hardly keep them open as something warm and wet was plopped into my arms.

A little girl.

Lance was beside me. I leaned my exhausted body against him and muttered, "Definitely your kid. Big head."

He laughed and kissed the top of my head, his arm wrapped around my shoulders. I let his strength surround me, breathed in his musky scent. Being with him revived me somewhat, and I tilted my head up to kiss his chin.

Lance kissed my lips, the taste of him warm and sweet. Looking down at our little girl, he whispered, "She's perfect." Her hair was so dark, slicked to her head with fluids, and her eyes were so vibrant and deep. She looked every bit like her daddy.

"She is," I agreed, offering her my finger. She wrapped her entire hand around my finger, but I knew that I was the one who was going to be wrapped around her.

For a brief moment, all the stress fell away, and I was able to focus on the here and now. My baby and my love. My family.

We'd come this far. We could go further. Love sure as hell wasn't easy, but I knew we could do it.

Epilogue

It was a year of firsts.

First honeymoon.

First baby laugh. First baby tooth.

First diaper change.

First steps.

Not necessarily in that order, because there sure as hell wasn't any order in the life I lived with Lance and our daughter, Hannah, ... and Spot and Dottie, and their three daughters and four sons: Speckle, Splotch, Dapple, Patches, Smudge, Splash, and Kitty.

If you couldn't tell, Lance named six of the pups, and Hannah named the last one, which was coincidentally her first word. Kitty turned out to be a boy, and —surprisingly — was not a cat, but whatever.

We lived in Northern California now, surrounded by the forests and mountains we had fallen in love with during our seven months of hiding.

Pooling our money, Lance and I had bought the perfect location to make my dream come true. The store wouldn't be open for a while yet, but I spent a lot of time there, like today, making plans and organizing everything.

There were a lot of smaller townships up here, which would make running a pet store difficult, but I was pretty sure I could make it work out. After all, most of the money made at pet stores was from food, accessories, and grooming, not from the animals sold there.

In the meantime, Lance had taken a job as a forest ranger. He was up early and home by dark. It worked for us.

As for Patrick, he had been found dead less than an hour after I gave birth to Hannah. He ran out into traffic while being pursued by a concerned citizen who had noticed the blood on his clothes. Whether it was an accident or suicide was never determined.

To me, it was all a tragic accident. Patrick really had seemed to believe what he was doing was the right thing. It had just come out in the wrong way, and only grew worse as time went on.

"What are you thinking about?"

I looked up at Lance, who was walking through our store with a box of supplies in his arms. Being a rather helpful child, Hannah was hanging onto his leg and chanting, "Go, go, go, go, go!"

I smiled at him. "Just the past."

He grunted and waddled off, swinging his leg out wide in front of him to make Hannah squeal. Seven tiny puppies scampered along behind the two of them. Only five weeks old, they still had a lot of growing left to do before they were ready to go to new homes. We'd already picked out all those homes, including one for Kitty, who would be staying right here.

I turned back to what I was doing, which involved sorting through more supplies. Dottie was on my right, Spot on the left. You could hardly see the scar from where he'd been shot, although he had a permanent limp. He liked to relax more than he used to.

Hadn't stopped him from making puppies, though.

Myself, I was pretty sure I had a puppy on the way, too. I'd been feeling a little odd, and I was waiting for some more time to pass, to see if the symptoms went away or not.

I was happier than I had ever been, despite taking a longer time to reach my goals than I would have liked. My parents hadn't talked to me since the day I told them off, but that was okay.

I had everything I could ever need right here.

The End